LILY
and the
LOST BOY

LILY
and the
LOST
BOY

PAULA FOX

A Yearling Book

Published by
Dell Publishing
a division of
Bantam Doubleday Dell Publishing Group, Inc.
1540 Broadway
New York, New York 10036

ISBN: 0-440-40235-2

Reprinted by arrangement with Orchard Books, a division of Franklin Watts, Inc.

Printed in the United States of America

November 1989

10 9 8 7 6 5 4

OPM

For
William Weaver
and
Floriano Vecchi

ONE

AT THEIR first sight of the boy, the two children forgot they were in a foreign place. It must have been that after living three months on the Greek island of Thasos, much of its strangeness had worn off and the island had become home to them. It was he who looked foreign.

He was standing motionless fifty yards or so up the path that led to the acropolis, the ancient stronghold whose ruins lay among a small forest of pine on the crest of a hill far above the coastal village of Limena where they lived. His bandaged right hand rested on a section of the great wall that had once enclosed the three hills around the village. He was glaring fiercely at something behind them. They turned to look.

What they saw appeared to be suspended between the sky and the Aegean Sea, which was pale blue now in midafternoon, though it would change color as the light changed and the day drew toward nightfall. Fishing boats swung gently at anchor, their night's catch long since delivered to the tavernas and restaurants on the waterfront. A quarter of a mile out beyond the small harbor directly below them was a tiny island that looked like a stroke of dark green crayon. It was too hazy to see the mountains of Macedonia on the mainland, two hours away by ferry.

"What is he staring at?" Lily Corey asked her brother, Paul.

"Nothing I can see," he replied.

"There's our house down there," Lily said.

"You always say that. Talk in a low voice."

"Why should I?" she demanded.

They turned back to the hill. "He hasn't moved," Paul said. "Maybe there's a viper near his feet."

"Why are you whispering? Let's go home."

"Wait!" he commanded.

"Now he's seen us!"

"He's only a kid," Paul said in a louder voice. "I can see him now."

"He's awfully tall," she noted.

"Look at his T-shirt. He's probably American."

"Everybody wears T-shirts," said Lily. "Even the snakes wear T-shirts—"

"—and a baseball cap," Paul interrupted, pushing her up the path. "Let's go meet him."

"What about the vipers?" Lily asked, shivering.

"I said one viper. You know they don't attack people, Lily."

"They think about attacking."

"Snakes don't think," Paul said impatiently.

"How do you know? On this island, even the rocks think."

"He's coming," Paul said.

"See you later," Lily said and headed down the hill. She didn't understand why she didn't care to meet the boy. Because of the vipers she usually picked her way along the hill paths, staring hard at the ground. Now she ran. The tiled roofs and cobbled lanes of the village seemed to rush up toward her, its flowers and trees like a huge bouquet into which she could press her face.

Lily was nearly twelve. Until she had come to Thasos, she hadn't often been scared in broad daylight. But there were places and things on the island that made her skin prickle and her heart beat loudly. Yet she loved it more than any place she had ever been.

She stopped to wait for Paul at a spot where a nanny goat was tethered. She had been afraid of that boy. Was it because he was a stranger? Except for shepherds and their small flocks of sheep, Paul and she were used to having the hills to themselves. Or was it because he'd looked so wild and white-faced and seemed to be coming from the acropolis, a haunted place to her?

Lily had gone there only once with Paul. They had clambered over fallen columns and stared into deep holes that had been chambers in the old times. It had been so still, so hot. A faded sign on a post had warned people not to walk beyond the acropolis to the steep edge of the hill, where they might slip on pine needles and plunge down to the sea far below. She had glimpsed the sudden movement of an animal as it disappeared between two great hewn stones. She had heard that young travelers who lacked money for a room would sleep there. Some of the Greeks in the village jokingly called it the Hotel Acropol.

The nanny goat bleated and came toward her as far as its tether would allow. She scratched its knobby head. Its eyes were like two immense almonds laid side by side. They reminded her of the eyes that gazed from the heads of the oldest statues in the Limena museum. After a minute or so the goat lost interest in her and began to graze. No viper would linger near a goat's hooves, so Lily sat down on the ground. Gradually, she felt herself fill up with the quietness that, like the scariness, was something new in her life.

At home in Williamstown, Massachusetts, she was always waiting for the school day to end, for Friday to come, for summer, for holidays, for television programs and movies and birthdays. But here, on this island in the north Aegean Sea, she didn't wait for anything. Each moment was enough in itself.

Had Paul's excitement at seeing the boy reminded her of all that waiting?

She pressed her sneakers up against a stone. Beyond it grew a patch of thistles. Beyond that was a path to the theater, a place so old it hardly seemed the work of human beings. The great apron of the stage was overgrown with wild flowers, and the marble benches that rose in steps against the hillside had been partly dislodged by ilex trees.

Still farther, olive trees grew in circular terraces, halted in their downward march by the roofs of Limena. And everywhere in those hills, still startling her when she came upon them, were sections of the marble wall built twenty-five hundred years ago, rearing out of the earth like dolphins from the sea.

The cloth of her jeans was warmed by the sun. She sniffed at the smells of wild thyme and rosemary. She turned so she could look down into the harbor. Visible at this time of day, glimmering in the water like bones, were the remains of an ancient shipyard that had been in use when thousands of people had lived at the foot of the hills instead of the few hundred who lived there now. A ten-minute walk away was another harbor, where ferries from the mainland docked. Just behind the ferry piers was a broad quay where fishermen mended their nets and the villagers strolled in the evenings. There was Giorgi's taverna facing the piers; late at night it was always filled with people who came to see the village men dance. Near it, leaning against a rough wood fence, were a dozen rusty old bicycles that a fat, sleepy-looking man rented to anyone who had a few drachmas to pay. The village boys, including Paul, rode them furiously about the quay until some grown-up, perhaps one of the village policemen, made them stop.

She could see nearly the whole village. Her own roof was like a beacon among the rooftops. Wherever she was wandering with Paul in the hills, she would pause to look for it and its untended garden that descended in terraces to the Temple of Poseidon, where chickens scratched among tethered goats and fishermen's wives hung their wash to dry on cords strung from stakes stuck in the ground amid the fallen columns.

Old and new were side by side in Thasos—a puzzle of time. A team of French archaeologists, who came every summer to the island, had arrived last week. It was their work to find parts of that puzzle and fit them into time. She spotted two of them now, digging in a corner of the old marketplace, the agora. Then she grinned to herself and stood up.

She'd seen, at the back of her house, a familiar head of dark, curly hair. It was her mother, standing beneath a mulberry tree and washing clothes in a large basin. Lily saw her pause in her work and look out to sea. She and Paul and people in the village often did that—look out at the water as though it might speak if you stared at it long enough.

She heard the thud of feet on the path and turned to Paul as he skidded to a stop next to her.

"He is American, and he lives up the mountain in Panagia," he said. His cheeks were flushed; he was smiling. The goat bleated once. Lily's heart fell.

They had grown close during these last months. Paul was nearly fourteen, but it was as though they'd become the same age. She knew it was partly because there hadn't been any ordinary days since they'd left Williamstown and partly because nothing was familiar.

In a family you got so used to everyone you didn't think about them anymore as separate people, and so used to daily life you didn't think much about that either. Here on this island he'd become her fellow-explorer, quick to see what she might have missed, who let her read aloud to him from her book of myths, who met her in the kitchen late at night when everyone was sleeping and made her cups of tea and canned milk.

"Why was he staring in that crazy way? Did you ask him what he was looking at?"

"He's training himself not to blink in sunlight," Paul replied.

"Great!"

"Lily, don't sneer at what you don't know about."

"Oh, let's go home," she said crossly.

"His name is Jack Hemmings," Paul said. "His father has a motorcycle. They go everywhere on it—Turkey, Thessalonika, all over the island. His father is a great dancer—the Greeks say he's the best on the island—and he writes poetry sometimes. Jack can speak Greek perfectly. They've lived here almost a year. Do you know what he did? What nerve! He slept in the acropolis last night. He can walk up the mountain to Panagia in just over an hour. That's eight kilometers."

Lily started down the path, Paul following her.

"What about his mother?" she asked, not looking around, not wanting to see in his face that eagerness that had nothing to do with her.

"I don't know. Maybe she and his father are divorced. I asked him, and he said. 'Oh, her . . . she's somewhere in Texas.' "

"What was the matter with his hand?"

"He fell on a rock in the acropolis. The cut bled for an hour, but he didn't tell anyone about it."

"He told you."

Paul was silent a moment. Lily knew she had a quick tongue, knew she was what her father described as being too fast on the uptake. When she was feeling mean, as she was now, she knew she could confuse Paul and make him uneasy.

"Well, I asked him," he said defensively. "You'd like him, Lily. He's smart. Sometimes he takes tourists to the ancient remains and gets paid for it. He's been out on a fishing boat, and he caught an octopus."

"So did you," she said. "What was he doing? Trying to get a job with you?"

He laughed at that. Her irritation with him suddenly went.

"He's going to take us places we haven't seen," he said. "We're supposed to meet him tonight at the Gate of Herakles, around eleven, he said."

"Mom will love that," she remarked. She hesitated, then she asked, "Did he say I should come?"

"Mom doesn't worry if we go out for a while at night. It's not like at home. We'll go after they're asleep."

He hadn't answered her question. She guessed that Jack whatever-his-name-was hadn't said a word about her.

A faint cry drifted up to them from the village. It sounded like "Yawurti! Yawurti!"

It was the boy who sold fresh yogurt. Lily and Paul

had stopped him one afternoon as he wheeled his bicycle on the quay. He'd opened the cover of a wooden box attached to the handlebars. Inside it were white bowls filled with yogurt. Paul told him they didn't have any dishes with them. He'd grinned and said if they'd open their mouths, he'd feed them yogurt until they ran out of drachmas. He was the cobbler's son, and like most of the young people in Limena he worked.

Lily wished she had a job herself. Even though Paul had included her in his intention to meet Jack tonight, she suspected things would change between them. There might be fewer myth readings in the kitchen over cups of sweet, tepid tea, fewer of the musing conversations they carried on in all of their roaming, talk that was filled with surprises for both of them, as though there had been barriers between them back home that had melted away beneath the flooding sunlight of the island.

TWO

PAUL CAUGHT UP with Lily where the hill path joined another broader path that was steep and stony. They moved down it cautiously, keeping their eyes on their feet. When they reached the rough stone steps where the village began, Paul said, "It was a relief, speaking English to someone."

"What have we been speaking? Duck?" Lily asked.

"Duck!" Paul shouted and burst into laughter. "Quack! Quack!" he cried.

As though in response an elderly couple called out greetings to them from a fenced-in garden. The children called back, "Yes, we're fine. And you?" Lily peered past the gourds which hung from the fence like small yellow moons. The old people would be taking their ease before starting to cook their evening meal. It was hard to find them among all the roses and dahlias, the fig and damson plum trees that filled their garden. She saw a pale hand waving among the green leaves.

"You know what I mean," Paul said. And she did know. Though she learned new Greek words every day, it was often a strain stumbling around in a new language, especially one for which you had to learn a new alphabet, too.

One of the reasons Mr. and Mrs. Corey had chosen the island was that they'd guessed there wouldn't be any English-speaking tourists visiting it. Such tourists, her father had said, drove up the cost of things because they wanted big hotels and nightclubs and tennis courts. There were tour ships that occasionally anchored off the island and sent sightseers ashore in small boats, but they usually stayed only a few hours. The Greek families who spent their vacations in Limena appeared to like the island the way it was. Mr. Corey had hoped they would all learn the language—and had been rather solemn about it. The funny thing was, he was hardly able to speak it himself, though he studied a grammar book for hours every afternoon. "I've become a prisoner of grammar," he'd said once to Mrs. Corey. "Throw me some nouns, Kathleen. I'm drowning in the passive subjunctive!"

Mr. Corey was a history teacher, and he was finishing a book on the Children's Crusade. It was because he had a sabbatical that they were able to come to Thasos for a few months.

When Lily thought about home—not very often—it was her room she pictured. From the window she could see two maple trees, a long-forgotten croquet wicket rusting on the lawn, and a narrow stream that dried up in summer. She had come to feel they had always lived on the island, and her room at home was like a snapshot in an album. She had had a hint of that feeling from the day in April when they had stepped off the small ferry from Kavalla onto the wharf and stood there, all of them blinking in the brilliant light, their suitcases piled around them. They had stayed for a few days in a small hotel. On her first morning there Lily had looked out a window and seen, not a stream, a croquet wicket, and two maples but a tall shepherd leaning on his crook, standing among a flock of sheep, behind him the steep rise of a mountain on whose lower flank old, thick-trunked olive trees seemed to whirl like dancers.

Then Mr. Kalligas had found them a house to rent. He had strolled over to them one evening as they sat around a table at Giorgi's taverna, introduced himself, sat down, and spoken to them in his quick, odd English, which, he told them, he'd learned during the years he'd been a cook in the British navy. It was clear from that first meeting that he'd appointed himself their guide and friend on Thasos.

"Come *on*, Lily!" exclaimed Paul. "You're dreaming."

He hadn't spoken to her so impatiently in a long while. "As if you didn't stand around half the day like an owl," she said sharply.

"There's Mr. Kalligas," Paul said. Far down the path, she saw the old man in the dark blue suit he always wore. He was making his way around the temple of Dionysus, carrying a platter covered with a cloth. He would be taking a roast home from the baker. The Coreys too, like almost everyone in the village, took their roasts to the baker to cook in his large oven. Only bread was baked in the small clay ovens people had in their yards.

They reached a high wall beyond which was their own yard. "Wait!" warned Lily.

An ancient woman was dragging herself by her hands across the path to her house opposite the Coreys'. Behind her the pipe of a public water faucet poked out of the ground. Every afternoon she came to it to wash her feet. Lily heard her groaning and sighing. She looked like a long bundle of sticks tied together, quite like the sticks they had seen her gathering as she crept and crawled about in her own yard. It was her chore in her family, collecting firewood for their bread oven. Her great-great-granddaughter, Stella, told the Coreys she was 103 years old. Almost ten times her own age, Lily had figured, born in a time that was nearly as remote to her as the great marble wall.

Paul was fidgeting. Lily touched his hand. "Another minute," she said.

"Another hour," he grumbled.

"She'll get upset if she hears us."

The old, old woman spoke some mumbled words, as indistinct as though they'd risen through deep water. Her stiff body trembled now and then with the tremendous labor of dragging herself into her yard. The last they saw of her were her narrow feet, yellow and fragile as late autumn leaves. With a jerk of her shoulders, she pulled herself out of sight.

Lily and Paul went around the wall to a high filigreed-iron gate, and Lily yanked at a cord that lifted a latch. They ran in, and the gate clanged shut behind them. Along the wall meandered a huge wisteria, its whale-colored branches nearly hidden by cascades of purple blossoms. Everything looked good against a stone wall, Lily had decided. A few yards beyond the front door of their house, shading the uppermost terrace, stood a large mulberry tree under which Mr. and Mrs. Corey sometimes read in the afternoons. Mulberries could stain, but the tree had been divested of its fruit since the morning a group of women had come to Paul and asked him to climb up among its branches and shake them as hard as he could. They had spread large cloths to catch the berries as they rained down and had taken them away to make preserves.

Lily loved to wander, but she loved coming home, too. The wild beauty of the garden still startled her. New flowers were always blooming; fruit swelled and ripened on apricot and peach trees. She didn't venture down to the lowest terrace. She was sure there were snakes there, coiling and uncoiling in all the tangle of bush and grass. She imagined Jack visiting. He and Paul would leap from terrace to terrace and laugh at Lily and her fears.

The front door was open as usual. One morning when someone had forgotten to close the gate, five goats had run into the long hall that went from one end of the house to the other, and had raced, their hooves clattering, into Lily's room just as she was putting on her socks. Bleating, their bells jingling, they had jumped through her window and out into the yard.

People came to visit with no more advance notice than the goats. Cousins of the woman who had rented them their house had come one day and spent the afternoon, drinking coffee, smiling at Mrs. Corey as she tried to make sentences from nouns, and looking sympathetically at Mr. Corey as he struggled to produce a small, correct sequence of words. Stella came too, when she could spare an hour from her large family, and Mr. Kalligas, of course. Mr. Corey was especially happy to see Mr. Kalligas, with whom he could speak English. Mrs. Corey fared better with Greek; she wasn't afraid of making mistakes. Their neighbors and the butcher, the baker, and Mr. Xenophon, who owned a small grocery store where the Coreys shopped, seemed delighted by her efforts.

Paul and Lily walked into the cool dark hall as their mother crossed it to the kitchen.

"Mom, there's another American on the island," Paul said.

"That's nice. After all, it's not our island," Mrs. Corey said. She was cranky, Lily guessed, because of the supper problem. Except for breakfast, meals took a good deal of thought. The children followed her into the kitchen. On an oilcloth-covered table lay a large bowl of strawberries.

"If we could only live on strawberries and honey and eggplant and bread," Mrs. Corey said, sighing.

"And Swiss canned milk," said Lily. Though both the children liked goat cheese and yogurt, they couldn't get down goat's milk.

Mrs. Corey was staring at the stove. It sat on a stone

shelf in a niche. It had two burners and an extra tiny one for making Turkish coffee. Except when they went to a restaurant, most of what they ate was fried or stewed.

"There are eggs," Paul reminded her.

"And chocolate," added Lily.

"It's the main dish that's hard," their mother said.

Mr. Corey walked in through the back door.

"I've finally solved that problem," he said. "I've built a barbecue pit."

They all went to look. Beneath the washing line, which stretched from a branch of the mulberry tree to a wooden post, Mr. Corey had dug a hole. He'd surrounded it with stones and laid a wire mesh across it. Inside the hole were twigs and tight rolls of newspaper.

"And I bought hamburger. At least I think that's what it is," he said. "It took me two hours and five hundred grammar mistakes to get the mesh. I think in one shop I asked for a bale of hay, but Mr. Kalligas came along and rescued me."

"We'll be able to grill fish and chicken," Mrs. Corey said. "Wonderful! Only now I'll have to learn the names of fish."

"We must learn everything well," Mr. Corey said.

Paul made a gargoyle face at Lily.

"If a fly goes by, your face will stick that way," their father observed.

"Lily, take in your clothes. They're dry." Mrs. Corey pointed to the washline. Hanging next to Lily's cotton skirt and blouse on the line was the octopus Paul had caught that morning, fishing from the breakwater in the harbor. When it was completely dried out by the sun, you could eat it. Like goat's milk, it was a thing Lily didn't care for.

She took her clothes to her room and stood for a moment at her window. The fire was burning brightly beneath the mesh. Darkness was spreading over the vast sky, coming, Lily imagined, from a huge smoke pot somewhere in Turkey. And the sea was the color of dark wine, just as Homer had described it in *The Odyssey*. The flames leaped, then subsided. She looked at the faces of her brother and mother and father. They were smiling, their expressions expectant as they looked down at the meat Mr. Corey had placed on the mesh. Her family! She thought she would always remember how they looked at that moment.

There was movement along the top of the wall. Many of their neighbors, including Stella, were lined up along it, gazing down at them in amusement. Stella said something and everyone laughed.

When the meat was cooked and put on a plate, the neighbors all waved at the Coreys, wished them a good dinner, and went away. At the kitchen table Mr. Corey said, "They were laughing because only barbarians would cook meat outdoors."

"They weren't laughing meanly. They don't do that," Mrs. Corey said.

"Perhaps not, but they must think us strange," said Mr. Corey.

Lily had nearly forgotten the taste of hamburgers. In the coming winter, when they were gathered around the table at home for supper, far from the honeyed air of Thasos, they might be eating hamburgers, speaking about this very moment. Thinking of that time in the future, she felt a touch of dizziness.

"No ketchup," complained Paul.

"No piccalilli," their mother said.

"Piccalilli is an Indian condiment," observed their father.

"You're always teaching, Papa," said Lily.

"Not when I eat strawberries," Mr. Corey said.

"What would happen if you couldn't remember anything?" Lily asked pensively. They all looked at her.

"I can't think of much worse than that," Mrs. Corey said.

"You wouldn't be able to learn—or teach," said Mr. Corey.

"But you wouldn't be afraid of going to the acropolis, Lily," Paul said, "because you'd forget about the vipers."

"I'd forget about the acropolis, too," Lily remarked.

After Paul had washed the dishes in hot water Mrs. Corey heated on the stove, and Lily had dried them and put them away on a shelf, Lily went to the balcony. She sat down in one of the two canvas chairs and looked out at the night. Moonlight silvered the brush and trees. In the Temple of Poseidon goats and chickens would be asleep now. The fishing fleet, its lights twinkling, was far out on the water. A distant murmur rose from the long row of stone buildings that were called the fishermen's houses, though not everyone who lived in them was a fisherman. Amber lights, glowing along the wharf and in front of tavernas, pulsed like little heartbeats, the heartbeats of rabbits throbbing away inside the dark. When the moon was full, its radiance dimmed all other light and picked out as though with silver ink every broken column, the stones of the breakwater, the huddled shapes of houses. Tonight thin splinters of black clouds drifted across the sky. The island of Thasopoula glittered like a tangled string of black beads.

Lily had read about Thasus in her book of myths. He was the grandson of Poseidon and was said to be the first colonizer of Thasos. Perhaps, she thought, his spirit lived on in that tiny island, watching Limena as it changed over thousands of years from a city of eighty thousand people to a small village, itself only the topmost layer of many layers of settlements going all the way down to that great city.

Often the Coreys went to swim from the rocks on the other side of the village. To reach them, they crossed a high, narrow embankment beyond the fishermen's houses. From the embankment Lily had looked down thirty feet or so to part of the ancient city and seen marble streets, the walls of stores, and ceremonial arches, some still half-hidden by the earth that had piled up over centuries. When she looked back to the path they were on, she saw small white houses, their gardens, a single street lamp at the end of the embankment, and once the yogurt boy's bicycle leaning against a wall—everything that was of this moment perched on the edge of the past.

Her father had turned on their small battery radio in the kitchen, and Lily heard the high wail of Turkish music. Sometimes her father tried to find an English-speaking station to hear news, though he was less interested in it than when they'd first arrived on the island.

Paul came out on the balcony and sprawled in the other chair.

"They're going for a walk soon," he reported. "I hope they don't stay out late."

She and Paul often went out at night but only for a short while, staying pretty close to the house. The idea of going all the way to the Gate of Herakles worried her.

A donkey brayed somewhere in the hills behind the village. Another donkey answered it from closer by. Paul began to sing in a whining voice, imitating the Turkish song.

"I don't see why we couldn't meet him in the daytime," Lily said.

"It's better at night," Paul said. She had a sudden vision of herself in front of their house in Williamstown. She and some friends were shouting and running in the street, in and out of pools of light cast by street lamps. To shout wildly and laugh, to run, were things you wanted to do on a summer night when the grown-ups let go of you for a while, and familiar things were in shadow.

"They might look for us later and be worried if we're not here," she said.

"They never wake up," he said. "Even when we've dropped things in the kitchen."

"I still don't see—" she began. But Paul brayed like a donkey and pulled her from the chair and pushed her into her room. The radio was off, and Lily, hearing the gate clang, knew her parents had gone for their evening stroll.

She and Paul sat on the floor and played cards. There were only two tables in the house, one in the kitchen and one in the room where Mr. Corey worked. Lily had grown to like the bareness of the rooms.

Paul won every rummy game. She didn't mind. At home her face would have turned red, and she would have been furious. He would have jeered and danced around her, holding up his hand like the champion. It was part of the difference of the way they were with each other here.

"Time for bed, children," Mr. Corey said from the doorway.

They had to brush their teeth at the kitchen sink. Once Lily had discovered three huge slugs the color of bruises clumped around the drain. They had come through the kitchen window. She had seen their slimy trails in the morning through the grass. The Coreys took baths in the kitchen, too—sponge baths, their mother called them— with hot water heated on the stove. Their house had an inside toilet of sorts, unlike many of the village houses. It was in a narrow room with a high window. You flushed it by pouring in a jug of water. They had found a dozen large terra-cotta jugs in the musty cellar.

Lily got into bed and took up her book. She had started to read about the Minotaur and Ariadne and Theseus. The murmur of her parents' voices came from the balcony, comforting like the babble of a stream. Suddenly Mrs. Corey's voice rose. "It does worry me," she said. "Not for Lily. She'll catch up. But Paul was close to failing math. Missing those months of school—" Her voice dropped.

Lily couldn't hear her father's reply. She could guess what he'd say. Even though he talked so much about the importance of school, he would declare that living here was the chance of a lifetime. "It is a golden place," he'd told Lily once. Someone else had said that, the only other American she had met on Thasos besides Jack Hemmings.

He had been a tall, skinny man, like a scarecrow in his crisp summer suit, his skin dry and brown as a paper bag. He'd been standing in front of the museum looking down the path to a huge stone statue of a youth with a ram slung around his shoulders. As she walked by, he turned and stared at her.

"I can tell by your long yellow braid that you're an American," he'd said in English.

She'd said she could be Finnish.

"Aha! Not with that accent," he'd replied.

He told her he worked for an American company in Istanbul, and always came to Thasos for his leave. "It's a golden island—Eden," he said.

"Except for vipers," Lily remarked.

"Oh, but there was a snake in Eden, too. So you see, it *is* perfect. For the moment, at least."

The book fell from her hand. She yawned and leaned over the edge of the bed to turn off the small shadeless lamp on the floor. She sank gently into sleep, sinking down through all the villages to a great marble city, and waking, in her dream, in another time.

Then Paul was shaking her foot, whispering, "Lily! Wake up! Let's go!"

It was hard to get out of bed, but his words gave her energy. At home he wouldn't have said, "Let's go." He would have said, "Take off! I'm busy."

She pulled on a T-shirt and slacks and slipped into her sandals. They went out the kitchen door, Lily shuddering at the thought of stepping on a slug, and around the house to the gate. Paul opened it carefully so as to not make any noise. Lily heard the public faucet dripping as they passed it on their way down to the center of the village.

When they came to the shrine of Dionysus, where the path became a street, she saw that her father had left their garbage there, as he did once a week, wrapped in a sheet of the Kavalla newspaper in front of the steps.

THREE

"Who takes the garbage away?" Lily had asked Stella, who was the one who had told them to leave theirs at the shrine.

"Someone comes at night," Stella replied vaguely.

The Coreys were the only family in their part of the village who had garbage to leave. Tonight a donkey was tethered close to the broad steps of the shrine and appeared to be staring down hopefully at the small package of empty milk cans. But when Lily was a few feet from the animal, she saw that its eyes were closed. The donkey's owner might be at Giorgi's taverna. When he came to collect it, he would take the cans too. The Greeks, Lily noticed, saved every piece of the slippery paper their meat and groceries were wrapped in and every piece of the string that secured the wrapping. Empty cans, she thought, must be especially valuable.

They passed the police station. A light glowed in one large window, and through it she saw the handsome policeman who always bowed so deeply to the Coreys when he met them. He was wearing dark glasses as usual and reading a newspaper.

Ahead of them was a long lane, parallel to the waterfront, leading to the main square. In front of all of the houses were pots of flowers, their colors deepened and darkened by the streetlights. A lean orange cat appeared suddenly from some hole, slunk along a few feet, and vanished. And at that moment the children heard the mandolin-like notes of a bouzouki, which fell into the late night hush like pebbles striking tin. Lily knew it was Dimitrious, the barber, playing in the taverna on the quay.

The Coreys had watched men dance to that strange music. They formed a circle, their arms around each other's waists. One or two would dance alone, their hands high in the air, clapping, sweat pouring down their faces. Mr. Kalligas urged Mr. Corey to join the circling men one night. The Greeks had clapped their hands and shouted encouragement, but Mr. Corey, shaking his head and smiling, had come up with the word *shy*, which amused everyone so much they forgot about persuading him to dance.

"What a triumph!" he had said later. "The only time I've used the right word at the right time." Mr. Kalligas had told them that same night about a foreigner, an American who lived in Panagia. "No one like him much but he is greatest dancer," Mr. Kalligas had said.

"Do you think Mr. Kalligas was talking about Jack's

father that time?" Lily asked Paul. But he was already turning down the street that would lead them east out of the village. She ran to catch up with him.

They passed the last streetlight. From there on the houses had no electricity, only oil lamps. She meant to ask him her question again, but she couldn't see his face. She felt a touch of fear as though she were alone on the dark road.

They came to a crossroads. One led up the great mountain to Panagia; another curved out of sight around a hill and led to a beach where they sometimes went to swim. Still a third led off to the western side of the mountain, where Lily had seen flocks of sheep grazing. From a distance they had looked like grains of rice scattered amid the sloping meadows.

The last village house stood by the crossroads. It was both a farm and a café. The Coreys had stopped there for cold lemonade on their way home from the beach. It was served to them by the young farmwife at one of three rickety tables in a yard beneath plane trees. Chickens scratched around their feet, and once a black goat no bigger than a puppy had leaped on their table and butted them with its hard little curly head.

Lily and Paul took the road to the beach and halted after a hundred yards. Against the hill stood an arch overgrown with vines. Columns glimmered among chestnut trees. It was a windless night, and the braying of a donkey seemed very close. Paul poked her in the ribs.

"Snakes come out at night," he whispered.

"Don't scare me," she begged.

"So you came," said a voice loudly from behind the arch. And Jack stepped out and jumped to the road. Lily gasped.

"Of course we did," said Paul.

"Since we saw you this afternoon, did you go all the way back to Panagia?" Lily asked.

He didn't answer her. "You didn't mention that you were bringing her along," he said to Paul.

When Paul said nothing, Lily spoke up with more confidence than she felt. "I go where I want to go," she said.

Jack glanced at a luminous wristwatch on his arm.

"In two minutes we can see the satellite passing," he said. "You have to have very good eyesight." He looked at Paul. "You know about it, don't you?" Paul shook his head. "It goes by this time every night."

Paul said, "You could have had supper at our house."

"I didn't need to," replied Jack. "I bought cheese and bread in the village and went back to the acropolis. I'm looking for old coins."

"Doesn't your father worry?" Lily asked. Without bothering to look at her, Jack said scornfully, "Why should he? Look! There it is!"

Lily and Paul looked straight up. A pinpoint of light— like the tiny light the eye doctor flashes in your eye— moved steadily across the sky and then was lost to view among the stars.

"That's it," said Jack. He was poised at the edge of the road in a ray of moonlight. There was something about his face that reminded Lily of the statue of the youth in the museum garden. Perhaps it was the faint smile on his lips that didn't change the expression around his deep-set eyes. His brows were dark and nearly met above his nose. He was much taller than Paul. A lock of his dark hair fell over his forehead. He pushed it back with his bandaged hand. Lily saw that the bandage was nothing but an old rag, a piece of soiled undershirt.

"How old are you?" she asked.

Paul pinched her elbow.

"Ninety-three," said Jack.

"I know a nice friend for you," Lily said. "She's a hundred and three." Paul snickered.

"I'm going to the beach," Jack said coldly. "I want to look inside that shack where the old woman cooks." He set off without a backward look.

"Why?" asked Lily. Paul, ignoring her question, followed him.

The shack was one of Lily's favorite places to have a meal. You didn't get much choice—fish or eggs and fried potatoes—but the potatoes were delicious and crisp, and the woman emptied them on your plate from a wire basket she had just lifted out of bubbling oil. A young fisherman brought her fish right out of the sea. When the Coreys sat there under the shade of an arbor with a grapevine climbing around it and they were salt-covered and damp-haired from the water, it always seemed a feast.

"I know what her kitchen looks like," Lily said. Jack was walking quickly, and Paul left her behind to catch up with him. Should she turn around and go home? She didn't. After crossing a low ridge of sand, the sea lay before them. A few yards out from the beach was the dark blot of an islet with scrub pine along its back. It huddled in the water like an animal at a water hole. She had swum out to it many times.

Jack broke into a run, stood for a second at the edge of the water, then ran in. "Come on!" he called back as he started to swim.

A dog barked once. It was not a sound you often heard in the village. As Lily had observed to Paul, it was hard for a dog to make a living in Limena. She knew that the lawyer who owned the dog (whose name was Rosa) lived around here in a house set back in the pines. Rosa wandered freely around the village and into tavernas, paid respectful attention by people because she belonged to an educated man.

"He walked right in with his clothes on," Paul said admiringly.

"Maybe he doesn't know the difference between water and air," Lily said.

"If you're going to be mean, why don't you go on home?" Paul asked her in a hard voice.

Jack stood up in the water, a dark shape except for his pale face. "It's a good way to wash your clothes," he called to them. Everything he does is good, *he* thinks, Lily told herself.

When Jack joined them, she saw the bandage was gone. There was a painful-looking gash on his hand. For a moment Jack stared at it, touched it with a finger, then shook his head as though to put it out of mind. He looks after himself, Lily thought, and he does what he wants to. But he's alone.

"The water is great," Jack said. "There're sharks, you know. A woman was torn to bits near Kavalla last week. Let's go look at that so-called restaurant."

"Nobody calls it a so-called restaurant," Lily muttered.

Rosa barked again. "I had a dog up in Panagia. But something got it in the night."

"What?" Paul asked.

"There are things it's best not to know," Jack said dramatically. Lily wondered if his father had said that. She tagged behind them as they walked up to the shack.

The woman closed up her shack at sunset. Lily had seen her put out the fire beneath the big pot and scatter the coals in the tile trench over which she fried fish and eggs. She would be home now, sleeping after her hard day's work.

"Can't we do something else?" Lily asked. They didn't answer her. She wished Rosa would come and chase them all away, but Rosa was such a mild creature she never chased anything. She was probably wagging her tail now, even as she barked, anticipating a social call.

Jack sat down at a table. "Service, here!" he called in a haughty voice. Paul laughed. She wouldn't be able to stop them from doing anything Jack thought up, Lily knew. She felt so troubled, thinking of the sleeping woman and feeling her own helplessness, that she almost wished she were home in Williamstown.

She stayed outside beneath the arbor while Jack and Paul went into the kitchen. On the chair where Jack had sat a puddle of water glimmered faintly in the starlight; she thought she heard his shoes squishing as he moved about the shack. Why had she tagged along with the two of them? Watery Jack and her brother made silly by him. There was a thud as though something had been knocked over.

"What a joint," Jack said, coming out. He turned to Paul, a step behind him. "We have to do something that will let her know someone has been here. Night customers."

"Why?" asked Lily.

"To show her," he replied indifferently, looking out at the sea.

"Show her what!" Lily demanded.

"Oh, Lily!" Paul burst out.

"Lily!" exclaimed Jack. "What a name!"

"I'm going home," Lily said.

"We'll turn the tables and chairs upside down—and take that pot into the woods—and why *don't* you go home?"

But Paul, to Lily's relief, said, "No. She goes home when I do." Jack stared at him, shrugged, and began to upend the tables. Paul turned over the chairs.

"We'll get the pot and hide it," Jack said.

Again Paul said, "No."

Jack drew back his foot and kicked up the sand. "Why not?" he asked challengingly.

"She makes her living here," Paul replied.

"Living!" he snorted. He looked at the upended tables and chairs. "It isn't enough," he said flatly.

"It *is* enough!" cried Lily. "You said you wanted her to know someone had been here. She will now. Paul, listen. Mom may get up and look for us. We ought to go."

"All right," he said. She saw him glance quickly at Jack. She suspected he was worried that Jack would think he did what she told him. "I was about to say we have to go. I have to get up early," he said.

"It's all the same to me," Jack said quickly. "I have a long walk up the mountain. It'll be dark as a pit."

"I'd be scared," Paul said. He held out his hand as though to offer Jack something.

"Of what?" Jack scoffed. "I'm not scared of anything. You have to be careful. That's all. Some old English lady slipped on the pine needles up at the acropolis. And she fell into the sea. All she had to do was read the sign up there. People are stupid."

They left the shack and walked across the beach to the road. "You might step on a sleeping viper," Lily said to Jack.

"Not me. I've got eyes in the back of my head," he said.

"You don't have them in your feet," Lily snapped.

Their footsteps echoed along the road. Lily heard the tinkle of a bell. Sheep must be moving somewhere above on the hill.

"Do you ever go to villages on the other side of the island?" Paul asked.

"We can go anywhere," Jack replied. "We can go to Istanbul in a morning on my father's motorcycle."

Lily imagined the motorcycle, snorting like a rhinoceros along the quiet mountain roads. She looked up at the star-strewn sky until she grew dizzy. What if, when she got home, she found her room torn up, the bedclothes on the floor, her books scattered beneath the bed, the lamp on its side? She'd be angry and, if she didn't know who had done the damage, frightened. But perhaps the woman who owned the shack would only think—boys . . . boys up to mischief. Yet Lily was pretty sure that whatever the boys of Limena might do, they wouldn't mess up a place where a person worked. Life was too difficult on the island. She didn't know exactly when she'd begun to realize that, maybe watching the ancient woman painfully gathering up twigs in Stella's yard.

"Next time we'll rent a boat," Jack was saying. "There's a sunken village an hour or two away from Limena. There was an earthquake years ago and a piece of the island sank down and took this little village with it. You row right over it, and you can look through the water at houses and a street and skeletons."

"Have you seen it?" Lily asked, interested despite herself.

"I heard about it from a person I trust," he answered loftily.

"Your father?" she asked. Jack said nothing.

"I'm going to Keramoti tomorrow with my friend Manolis and his father," Paul said.

"You didn't tell me that," Lily said.

"I don't tell you everything," Paul said sharply. He turned away from her to Jack. "His father makes those big jars almost like the old ones you see in the museum. He sells them on the mainland."

Jack yawned. "Sounds boring," he commented.

"How are you going to let us know when we can row over that sunken village?" Paul asked timidly. "I'd better tell you where we live."

They had reached the crossroads where the stone farmhouse stood.

"I know where you live," Jack said. "I've been watching. I'll leave a note under your gate." He paused for a moment. "It might be hard to get a boat. So meanwhile we can meet at the bicycle place."

Quite suddenly, he turned his back on Paul and Lily and strode up the road toward the mountain and Panagia.

"What a pill," she said.

"He is not," Paul whispered fiercely. "You don't know anything about him!"

"What do you know?" she demanded.

Paul looked up at the farmhouse. "You want to wake up everybody?"

"Going into the water like that, with all his clothes on. What was he trying to prove?"

"I don't know," Paul said uncertainly. "But he's not a pill."

Lily sighed. Her shoes were full of sand.

"Come on, let's go home," Paul said.

"Could we go back by the Silenus Gate?" she asked. "Maybe the satyr will wink at us."

"It takes too long that way. And it's superstition anyhow," Paul said, walking on down the road to the village.

"You went there with me before," Lily protested. She had heard from Mr. Kalligas that the satyr would wink if you waited long enough. She and Paul had gone to look at him one lazy afternoon when most of the people in the village were taking their afternoon rest. The satyr looked out of weathered, crumbling stone, grinning as though he was glad he'd ruined himself with pleasures, his fat face half-hidden by tendrils of vine.

The village was dark now. When they reached the shrine of Dionysus, Lily saw that the donkey and their garbage were gone. She went up the steps and touched a column. It was cool beneath her fingers.

"Lily!" Paul said.

"I feel bad," she said quickly. "I want to go back and put the tables and chairs right."

"I won't go," he said at once.

"I'll go alone," she said.

He started up the sloping path to home. She caught up with him, tried to see his face.

"It's not bad—having someone besides just us, to talk English with," he said.

"I guess so," she said halfheartedly. She understood there would be no use in arguing with him.

They tiptoed into the house and went to the kitchen. "I'm going to bed," Paul said. Lily turned on the light, an uncovered bulb hanging by a cord from the ceiling. It gave a faint ping, dimmed, and brightened again. The village generator wasn't very dependable.

"I'm going then," she said.

He went and peered into the sink, then turned and looked directly at her. "You don't have the nerve," he said.

"I'll go without nerve," she said.

He yawned hugely. "I'll believe that when I see it," he said. But he didn't wait to see anything, just walked out of the kitchen without another word.

Lily cut two pieces of bread and smeared them with honey. She would eat the sandwich when she reached the shack. It wasn't so far after all, a little over a mile. Nothing would happen to her. That time she'd fallen off a wall into a patch of nettles people had run out of their houses to help her. The farmer in the stone house would hear her cry out if she saw a snake. It will be a brave thing to do, she thought. And Lily wanted to be brave.

FOUR

A FAINT, LOW WIND—it seemed to strike her legs just below her knees—was the only sound Lily heard until her feet dislodged some pebbles near Dionysus' shrine. The wind dropped then, and the silence heaved up. Soon she turned east and in a few minutes had left the houses behind her. The dark was like a cat's thick fur pressing against her face.

As long as there had been houses, she held back the fear that had first come to her the time she and Paul and their parents had walked through a grove of the oldest olive trees in Limena.

Mr. Kalligas had taken them there to show them the remains of a Hellenistic cemetery. Gleaming white edges of marble tombs showed through the earth among clumps of lavender where bees hummed and fed. She and Paul had run ahead, bored with the way Mr. Kalligas would halt and, his hand pointing to a tomb, speak of a dozen things—his life in the British navy, the odd ways of tourists, his son and daughter far away, working at jobs in Germany.

Paul had suddenly shouted something—it must have been her name, he was looking at her so intently, gesturing at a huge olive tree that was so twisted it seemed it would uncoil like an overtightened spring at any moment. As Lily stared at it, she saw emerge from its hollow trunk two enormous vipers writhing in the air.

Her ankles went numb, then her legs.

"I can't move," she muttered to Paul. He gripped her arms and rocked her back and forth as though she were a doll. "They've gone! They dropped back inside the tree. It's okay, Lily. Lily!" After that she never looked at an olive tree without remembering what she had seen that day.

Her eyes grew accustomed to the dark. Her hearing sharpened. She heard a multitude of sounds: cicadas like small knives being sharpened rapidly on steel, the movements of animals across brush and over stones, vagrant breezes rising among the pines and chestnuts on the hill. The air was pungent with the smells of resin and wild herbs and flowers. As she turned toward the beach at the crossroads, she could see ahead the hunched, shoulder-like arch of Herakles. She wished there were a replica she could always carry with her of the immense eyes, supposed to ward off evil, that were carved on a slab of stone near the Parmenon gate.

The swish of her feet on the sand-dusted road made a

comforting sound. But she wouldn't have minded hearing a rooster crow or a donkey filling up the night with its rusty bray. She recited aloud the names of the ancient gates of Limena, startled at first by the sound of her own small voice. "Silenus, Herakles, Dionysus," she said. "Zeus and Hera, Hermes and the Graces, Parmenon . . ."

When she stepped onto the beach, she could see better. There were no trees and hills to obscure the starlight. The moon had set long ago. The lapping of water against the shore was peaceful, a dreamy sound. She went swiftly to the shack and began to right tables and chairs. They felt nearly weightless. Why had the boys' actions seemed to her so dreadful at the time?

There had been no real harm done. Yet she had been frightened, as though harm had been what they wanted to do. She thought back to the moment when Jack had said, "We have to do something so she'll know we've been here."

He hadn't meant leaving a bunch of flowers. He had determined to leave a sign that someone *wanted* the old woman who owned the shack to be distressed, alarmed. Why? She knew Paul hadn't much wanted to do it, yet he'd gone along with Jack.

She stood back. Everything was in its place. She had erased the sign Jack had left. She was no longer afraid; she felt calm at the prospect of the long walk home. The worst was over.

Then she froze. She had heard a sound very like a snore.

It came again, louder. Ghosts can't snore. And gods

wouldn't, would they? It was coming from inside the shack. She made herself move to the entrance into the kitchen. Her hand reached out. She felt the rough surface of the black pot. Near it on the earthen floor she saw the shape of the boy—Jack—asleep, his head resting on a bundle of cloth. Lily squatted down and stared at him.

He hadn't gone to Panagia. Why, she wondered, had he pretended he was going? She and Paul had seen him start up the mountain road with his pirate's swagger. But he had waited, hidden behind a tree probably, until they had left the crossroads, then returned. He said he'd taken cheese and bread to the acropolis, but that had been many hours ago. He wouldn't have eaten since then. Had he hoped there would be something to eat in the shack that he and Paul hadn't discovered? Was that the real reason he'd wanted to come in the first place?

From the scarf she'd wrapped around it, Lily took the bread and honey sandwich and placed it beside him, a few inches from his face. His snoring stopped. She moved quickly out of the shack. The snoring began again more softly. She was sure, suddenly, that his father had gone off somewhere on his motorcycle, leaving Jack to take care of himself. He groaned and muttered something.

She didn't like him, but she felt a pity for him that was nearly like anger—an unwilling pity. She stayed another few minutes, troubled by her contrary feelings about him, worried that her parents might wake and look for her. She imagined Jack waking up, finding the sandwich.

She turned and sped back to the road, hoping Rosa

wouldn't bark and wake him. There was a different quality to the dark; it was thinner, softer, fading even as she looked up at the hill. Far above, among the terraced olive trees, she could see clearly a flock of sheep, their dark muzzles pointed toward the sea. She whistled softly. The flock twitched like one large animal. The bellwether ram jerked itself up on its stiff legs, its bell tinkling, and began to move higher up on the hill. The rest of the flock followed him.

At the crossroads Lily looked up toward Panagia. The sun would soon touch the peak of Hypsarion, nearly four thousand feet high, and then the light would flow down the slopes like honey, across meadows and forests and waking flocks of sheep until, finally, it would penetrate the dark interior of the shack where Jack lay sleeping.

In the small courtyard of the farmhouse she caught the movement of a chick, like a streak of butter, as it rushed and veered beneath tables and chairs. Chickens, she thought, always assume human beings are out to get them—and with good reason.

The village felt alive as she entered it and passed the first houses. It was as though the soft, slow movement of people waking to another day was visible through the thick walls of their rooms. Though it was still dark in the west and the north, the mountains of Macedonia held arcs of light like crowns on their peaks. Then she saw the boats of the fishing fleet sailing across the calm water, their high prows bathed in the ever-growing light. The fishermen would soon jump to the wharf and shake out nets full of red and silver fish, and Giorgi and the other taverna owners would choose and buy what they would serve that day to their customers.

Mr. Xenophon must already be behind the closed door of his grocery. She couldn't hear him, but the table where he served his friends brandy was in its place beneath the baobob tree. As she went past the shrine of Dionysus, she heard the thin, penetrating sound of a shepherd's pipe.

Lily walked faster. She turned once and saw that the boats were now clustered just inside the harbor. The sea was olive green. It would soon be the hour when she and Paul were sent to the baker for breakfast bread and to Mrs. Christodoulou, who kept chickens, for eggs.

The piping seemed to come from the path on the hill where the nanny goat was tethered. It was hard to tell. The notes fell from everywhere like drops of rain. Lily saw Stella, yawning, emerge from her yard and look up toward the theater. A few yards beyond her stood two elderly sisters dressed in black. Lily knew that both of their husbands had drowned many years before when the fishing boat they were on capsized during a storm. They too were facing the hill. And other neighbors of the Coreys were gathering silently in front of their houses.

Just where the path narrowed, at the last house on the lane, stood a very tall old man. His clothes were tattered. A frayed rope held up his pants. His shoes appeared to be made out of some faded, feltlike cloth. Perched forward on his massive head and thick gray curls was a stained fedora hat, its brim turned down. He gripped his pipe with reddened fingers. His eyes were closed. The notes softened as though he were whispering his song. As Lily reached her gate, Stella turned, smiled, and silently held out her hand. Lily took it in hers, feeling the warm, calloused palm against her own. She had been very much alone the last two hours. She realized now, comforted by Stella's strong clasp, that she had been lonely too.

She glanced through the gate to her house. They must all be sleeping hard inside, their dreams barely stirred by the sound of the pipe. She probably wouldn't have heard the old piper either if she hadn't been out on the path. They were foreigners, after all. You'd have to live a long time in a place to recognize something out of the ordinary when the ordinary itself was so mysterious.

Stella pulled her gently along the path. The old man raised his head. Lily saw that his eyes were not shut but wide open and they were bluish white, the color of the midday sea. He was blind.

At that moment he ceased playing. He put out his hands, seemed to feel the air, nodded to himself, then spread his fingers as though blessing the people now gathered close to him. He began to speak in a deep, husky voice, and as he went on, words following each other as surely and as rapidly as had the notes of his pipe, he sounded to Lily like someone who tells a story learned by heart and recited over and over again. No one interrupted him or said anything at all, but now and then Lily saw someone smile or nod as though in agreement. After he had spoken for five minutes or so, he stopped abruptly and began to move down the path. His feet seemed to know every stone of it as well as his voice had known his story. People made way for him, staring at him pensively as though thinking over what he had told them. A few minutes later Lily heard the pipe again coming from near the shrine of Dionysus.

He was summoning another group of people, whose houses were near the shrine, Stella told Lily.

"Did you understand what he said?" she asked Lily. The others had returned to their houses, and she and Stella were standing by the gate. "A few words," Lily said. "That he slept on the ground and the night was black."

"Yes," Stella said, "but there was more." And she told Lily that the piper had had too much retsina wine the night before in Panagia where he lived. When he got home, his old wife had flown into a rage. She'd pummeled him and kicked him and finally driven him out into the black night and barred the door against him. He had had to sleep on the ground. His bones would ache for a week. He had come down the mountain to tell everyone what a misery his wife was. Young men contemplating marriage, he had warned, must consider a young woman's character. Was she merciful? Was she stronger than he was? Would she forgive him when he was old and weak?

"She has to forgive him often," Stella said, grinning. "We have all heard his story before. By the time he has told it to all of Limena and walked back to Panagia, she will have a pot of soup waiting for him."

"Doesn't she mind his telling everyone about her?"

"We all like to hear the story," Stella said. "He always

makes it different. No, she doesn't mind. She knows that after each journey down the mountain, he will be sober for a good long time."

⎍⎍⎍ Lily pulled down the cord and released the latch on the gate. The front door was ajar. She tiptoed into the hall and went to Paul's doorway. He was entirely covered by his blanket. By the small alarm clock on the floor next to his bed, she saw it was nearly six o'clock. She thought of all that had happened to her since she had left the kitchen in the dark of night. If you could stay awake twenty-four hours, you wouldn't miss a thing except your dreams.

Her parents' room was dark, the tall wood shutters closing out the light. She always loved to push them open. They swung out like sails, and the day poured in.

Light was what furnished their house, flooded the rooms that were empty except for a chair or two, their beds, and the baskets Mrs. Corey had bought in the village, in which they kept their clothes and bed linen and towels.

Although she was so tired she was stumbling, Lily went into the kitchen to get a piece of bread and cheese. She was even hungrier than sleepy.

Would Jack think a god had left him the bread and honey? What *would* he think? She suspected he would laugh at the old stories. A god hadn't left him food. She had. But then, maybe she had been *led* to leave him food by a god. She had cut herself a slice of bread and was about to take a piece of cheese from underneath the wire net where it was kept, when she heard a scrabbling noise from beneath the table. Nervously, she stooped down to look.

"A tortoise!" she whispered aloud. She picked it up. It tucked in its head and legs, and it just fit her palm.

"Where'd you get that?" Paul whispered from behind her. He was standing in the doorway in his pajamas, yawning. "It's the same color as the honey," she said. "It was under the table."

Paul walked over to the sink and turned on the faucet, filling his hand with water and gulping it down.

"It's just a snake with a shell instead of scales," he said.

"It is not!" she said. Some mornings started this way with both of them ready to be bad-tempered. She never understood why.

"You don't know everything," he said. "And you sure don't know about reptiles."

"I'm petting it," she said calmly. "I'm going to call it Glaucus. That's the name of a general whose cenotaph is in the agora." She paused and looked at her brother. "In case you don't know what cenotaph means, it means a tomb without a body."

"In case you don't know, there's a slug in the sink," he said.

Lily knew there were never slugs in the sink in the morning.

"A slug is a body without a tomb," Paul said.

"Lame," commented Lily. But he was grinning, and she giggled. The match was over for the moment.

"How come you're up so early?" he asked. "You didn't go back to the beach, did you? I can't believe it!"

"Well—I did," she said. She took out a piece of cheese and wrapped bread around it.

He looked at her with interest. "Did you get any sleep at all?"

"None," she said. She held out the tortoise. "I almost bit into Glaucus," she said. "Would you put him out in the yard?"

He took it from her and examined it closely. "We could keep it," he said.

"No—he was born free," she said. Paul laughed and took it out the back door. She watched from the window as he put the tortoise down beneath the mulberry tree. She was thinking about Jack, who might be awake by now.

If she told Paul she'd found him there in the shack, he would know Jack had lied, was hiding something—about his father or himself. Would it matter to Paul? She was confused suddenly. Why did it matter to her? Why not tell Paul in the usual way she told him things? Because she knew it wasn't usual; because she was worried. But did it matter to *her* what Jack did?

She had left him the sandwich partly from an impulse of mischief—to baffle him. But she'd pitied him too, asleep on the ground, snoring like an old person. What she was feeling now—at least, so she thought—was an odd protectiveness toward Jack. But she couldn't think against what.

"Did you put all the tables and chairs back the way they were?" Paul asked as he walked into the kitchen.

"I did. When I got back here a while ago, there was an old blind man playing a pipe. Didn't you hear him? He told the whole street a story about his wife locking him out of his house."

"I only heard you stomping around in the kitchen," he said.

She yawned. "Paul, would you get the bread and eggs this morning? I can't stay up another minute."

"What are you going to tell Mom?" he asked with an intent look at her.

"Oh, don't worry, I won't tell about your silly trick out there on the beach. I don't know what I'll tell her. Would you say I didn't sleep much last night and please don't wake me?"

Paul nodded. "Poor Jack," he murmured. "Going all the way up the mountain—"

"He's not poor Jack," she broke in angrily.

"Okay, okay . . ." he protested mildly, looking surprised.

She staggered into her room and sank down on her bed.

When she woke up, the sun was shining in her face through the window. A man was singing from far down on the last terrace.

It must be one of the village men who worked for the

archaeologists, she guessed. She knew they'd found a great stone archaic bird just a foot beneath the soil at that end of the garden. They must have started a dig there today to see what else they could find.

She changed her clothes and went down the hall. Her father was sitting at his table, smoking his pipe and staring at a closed book he held in one hand. There were chopping sounds coming from the kitchen. She felt as though a week had passed since she'd walked home from the beach.

"Well!" her mother exclaimed as Lily walked into the kitchen. "The sleeping beauty! You look flushed. You haven't got a fever, have you?"

She put her hand on Lily's forehead.

"Cool as a cucumber," she said and turned back to the table where she had been cutting up cucumbers and tomatoes.

"What are you making, Mom?"

"A cold soup," Mrs. Corey said. "Something I can make with the materials at hand. It's called gazpacho."

"What else is in it?"

"Oh, pork chops, bacon—the usual," said Mrs. Corey, grinning.

"Oh, Mom!" Lily said, smiling. She took an egg from a bowl, intending to hard-boil it.

"Lily?" her mother asked in a serious voice.

Lily kept her back to Mrs. Corey.

"I went in to look at you last night—"

"—to make sure I was covered," Lily interrupted, trying to delay what she knew was coming.

"Yes. And you weren't there. Where were you?"

"I couldn't sleep. I went out for a walk. A kind of long walk."

Her mother didn't speak for a few minutes. Lily filled the little blue Bulgarian saucepan with water.

"Lily, go out on the balcony when you can't sleep. Everything is very—very benevolent here. But I don't like the idea of you walking around in the middle of the night. Okay?"

"Okay," said Lily. She sighed. She wasn't sure whether it was from relief or regret.

FIVE

WHEN PAUL returned in midmorning from his trip to Keramoti with Manolis and his father, he wanted Lily to go with him at once to the acropolis.

"But what happened?" asked their father. "I mean— Paul! Think of it! For thousands of years Greeks have been sailing the Aegean, a cargo of those splendid storage jars in their ships' holds. And now you've done what they did—"

"It was just a big messy rowboat with a kerosene motor. When we got there, a couple of men helped unload the jars, and we came back," Paul said.

"Talk about understatement!" Mr. Corey exclaimed. "I'd like to hear your report on the Trojan War."

"Well—it wasn't much," Paul said flatly.

Mr. Corey, who had been smiling, looked faintly irritated.

"It's just daily work for Manolis' father," their mother said. "It always *has* been someone's daily work."

"Well . . ." began Mr. Corey dubiously.

"Speaking of work—" said Mrs. Corey, looking at him.

Mr. Corey sighed and went off to his desk table.

Lily was thinking about temples and shrines, about portals partially blocked by earth on which nameless carvers had left flowers and birds and the faces of beasts and men. When she traced with her fingers the letters of an ancient inscription on a stone or touched the shaft of a column, she sensed something else the workmen had left, more mysterious than daily work; something she could feel with the tips of her fingers but couldn't name, a thing that came from them across the centuries to her. It was as if she touched their hands.

"Lily, stop looking that way!" Paul exclaimed.

"What way?" she asked, startled out of her reverie.

"You look asleep with your eyes open. It's creepy."

"You should see how you look when you get up in the morning," Lily retorted. "Super-creep!"

"Now, children," their mother murmured as she went out into the yard.

"Come with me right now," Paul said to her urgently. She knew he hoped Jack would be at the acropolis.

"I hate to go up there," she said.

"You can take a book and sit on the path with the goat. Maybe I'll find some valuable coins."

"All right," she agreed reluctantly.

⌐⌐⌐⌐ For the next few days they went up the hill. Lily stayed by the nanny goat, reading. After an hour or so Paul would come slowly down the path.

"Any coins?" Lily would ask.

One morning he said in a discouraged voice, "I don't really know where to look."

"Okay. Let's do something else."

That afternoon she went down to the quay with him and sat under a plane tree while he and Manolis and the boys who could afford a few drachmas to rent them rode the battered bicycles back and forth along the water's edge. Girls didn't ride. She had rented a bike once, when they first came to the island. Just as she had taken hold of the handlebars, the handsome policeman had appeared from an alley leading to the quay and stood in front of her. He had smiled apologetically. "No, not for little girls," he had said gently. "Very dangerous."

She hadn't known enough Greek then to argue with him. Now that she did, she'd lost interest in riding. All the boys did was to shout and try to cut each other off. Most of them didn't speak to her. They look shyly at the ground when she greeted them. Only Manolis, and Nichos and Christos, the young sons of Costa, the museum keeper, exchanged a few words with her. On the evening promenade she had noticed that teenagers didn't mix unless a boy and girl were engaged to be married. Then they could walk together. People were kind and affectionate in

Limena—they hugged each other and kissed when they met—but there were some strict rules about the way you were supposed to behave that you found out only when you broke them.

Mr. Corey had hit a good work period and stayed at his table until late afternoon. The beach took too long to reach, so they went off to the rocks to swim, wearing their suits beneath their clothes. When they reached the embankment above the old city, Lily saw one of the French archaeologists. He waved to the Coreys, then squatted down to study something in the pile of dirt near his feet. It looked awfully far down to where he was.

"I saw you riding Christos on your handlebars here today," she said in a low voice to Paul. "You shouldn't do that. What if you fall?"

"Don't be a prune," he said. "I only did it once. Why don't you go hide in the cellar? You're so scared of everything."

"I'm scared of what's scary," Lily said.

"Aren't you great!"

"Yes, I am," she said, looking at him slyly out of the corner of her eye. She could tell by his face he was trying to think of something to say that would get her. But she had always had the last word, at least so far.

It was a lovely hour of the day. The wind would rise soon, as it did in the late afternoon, and blow away the heat. Shadows lengthened. The light lay in long golden swaths across the hills and village and on the fishing fleet, where the men were making things ready to depart at twilight. Flocks of homing birds flew swiftly toward the woods. People in the streets walked quickly, buoyantly, refreshed by the coolness, looking forward to their evening meals. As the Coreys scrambled down to the smooth, large rocks from which they could drop off into the water, Lily looked up the hill and saw a section of the marble wall gleaming among the pines.

Paul was the first one in, but he rose up almost at once with a watery cry, a grimace of pain on his face. He clambered up on a rock, hunkered down, and gripped his head. Mr. Corey pulled his hands away. Lily saw the black spine of a sea nettle sticking out of his hair. Mr. Corey pulled at it, and Paul let out a shriek.

They hurried back along the path toward home, Mrs. Corey, her arm around Paul's shoulders, promising she could take out the spine with tweezers.

Stella was washing down the stone walk to her house. She paused to ask Mrs. Corey what was wrong, and when she heard, she looked sympathetically at the groaning boy. She dropped the wet rags she had been using and said she knew exactly what to do.

In the Coreys' kitchen Stella made Paul sit down at the table. He was making an effort, Lily saw, not to cry. Stella went to the wire mesh where Mrs. Corey kept olives and cheese, took an olive, and heated it over the flame on the stove. When it was smoking, she dashed to Paul and pressed the olive on his head where the spine had entered. Paul howled. Then he looked surprised. Stella was holding up, for all of them to see, the smashed olive with the spine sticking out of it.

"It stopped hurting just like that!" Paul exclaimed.

"Have coffee with us?" Mrs. Corey asked Stella. She shook her head. She had to go home to finish her work. In the afternoons everyone in the village cleaned up their yards and washed down their stone paths and then themselves. When they appeared later in their gardens or on the quay, they looked sea-washed as though they'd just emerged from the Aegean.

"Saved by the olive," remarked Mr. Corey.

"It is beautiful here," Mrs. Corey said. "But so full of stinging, biting creatures. In fact, it's so dangerous, I feel like eating out tonight." She took Paul's hand and pressed it in her own.

"Could we go to the movie after supper?" he asked.

"The film breaks a dozen times, the children cry, the sound is fuzzy, and we've seen that awful movie twice," Mr. Corey protested.

"It sounds wonderful," Mrs. Corey said. "We'll see."

Lily went to her room and changed into the cotton dress she wore when they went out to eat. It seemed a little tight, though it had fit her a week ago. Flowers and trees grew so wildly on this island—perhaps she was growing wildly too.

People ate late in Limena, so Lily settled down with one of the books Mr. Corey had brought back from the American library in Kavalla a few weeks earlier. It was a history of the wars between Persia and Greece. It was often boring to her, but on Thasos, she was desperate for anything to read. The one thing that interested her in the book was the plight of the farmers. Whether it was the Greeks or the Persians who advanced across their land, the farmers always found themselves in the same fix, trying to hide their flocks and grain from soldiers. They hardly ever had time to complete a harvest, and when they did, the soldiers from both sides made off with all of it.

Paul wandered into her room.

"What do you think happened to him?" he asked. It was the first time in days he'd referred to Jack, even indirectly. Lily had been practicing forgetting him, and she had almost been successful.

"Maybe he and his father have gone back to wherever they came from," she answered with an indifference she didn't feel.

Paul's face fell.

"Or he's up in Panagia with his father," she added quickly.

"I guess he has friends there," Paul said.

"Well—you have friends here in Limena," Lily noted.

He stared at her but she wasn't sure he was seeing her.

"Do you think this dress is too tight?" she asked him.

"Ha-ha!" he cried. "Too tight! You look like a balloon in a Christmas stocking."

"Thanks."

"How do I know if it's too tight?" he asked. He picked up a deck of cards from the stone sill of the window and began to shuffle them. Lily went back to her book; the words were packed so tightly on the page, they looked like a mob of ants.

"What are you reading?" Paul asked.

"Herodotus," she answered. "About the wars between the Persians and the Greeks."

He looked rather sad as though she'd given him disappointing news.

"Listen, Jack will turn up," she said impulsively.

Paul was staring at the king of spades. "He's crazy," he said suddenly.

She was startled but said nothing.

"You want to play cards?" he asked.

"Okay. But don't get sore if I win."

"You won't win. And I never get sore."

The sky was darkening. Lily turned on the unshaded lamp on the floor. They played a few games. Paul began to look more cheerful. When a donkey brayed, he imitated it silently, opening his mouth wide and nodding his head up and down. A sudden breeze swept through the window, bringing with it the evening smells of Limena. Roses and chickens and squash flowers, Lily said to herself, and roasting lamb, dahlias, the black, tight smell of Turkish coffee, and the almost flower-like smell of the sea.

"And there's that piney smell," Paul said.

"You read my mind."

"I didn't, Lily. You're sniffing the air like Rosa does. It isn't hard to figure out. You want to make everything seem like magic . . . a mystery."

She pondered that for a moment, selecting a card from the pile on the floor.

"Everything is, in a way," she said as she laid down her hand, the ace of hearts she had just taken from the deck making a full run.

"You've destroyed my winning streak," Paul said.

"Magic," she said.

"It's only one hand. I'll allow it because I'm going to win anyhow."

She heard her mother laugh. She felt weightless, suddenly, buoyed up by happiness. It was lovely to go to the village in the evening, lovely to be greeted with a special evening gaiety by people whom they saw in the daytime. It wasn't that the food would be so wonderful at Efthymios' tiny restaurant where they usually went for supper. It was the cheerfulness of the place that drew the Coreys there. Its four tables would be set outside on the pavement Efthymios washed down every afternoon with buckets of cold water. There would be pots of geraniums at the door, and Efthymios, the chef and only waiter, his clean, frayed shirt open at the neck, would stand patiently beside the Coreys' table, waiting for them to tell him what they wanted—which he already knew since each of them always ordered the same thing. Lily would have pastitsio, macaroni and lamb in a sauce; Mr. Corey would have sardines fried in oil; Mrs. Corey would take the soup of beans and macaroni that had been cooking slowly for hours in the dark little kitchen; and Paul always chose the omelet. The restaurant was the smallest in Limena. For a joke, people called Efthymios "Onassis," which had been the name of a rich shipowner. In his placid way he appeared to enjoy the joke himself.

"Let's go, children," called Mr. Corey.

Paul played his last, and winning, card. "Once again!" he cried.

"How boring it must be for you," commented Lily.

"It's *never* boring to win," Paul said with a grin.

As they passed Dionysus' shrine Mr. Corey said, "It looked like this in the moonlight on an evening two thousand years ago."

"It couldn't have, Papa," said Lily. "It was new then. There were statues inside it, and the columns were standing."

"You could set yourself up as the local historian," said her father.

If they hadn't all been together, she would have spoken to him of the great banquet she had read about that had been given for Xerxes, the son of Darius the Persian, 2,462 years ago, probably close by where they were now walking. But she knew it would annoy Paul; he'd say she was showing off or being horribly boring. If they were by themselves, Paul seemed to like it when she told him something she had read about the place they were exploring. But not around their parents.

She thought she knew why—it was because she was a better student at school than Paul. Her mother had said once that Paul was often lost in dreams. But Paul didn't know it was difficult to be good at learning. It seemed to her that everyone felt sorry for people who were lost in dreams. Her parents weren't sorry for her. Now and then she made herself into a heavy lump and replied dully, "I dunno," when her father asked her what she was reading or studying these days. He'd just laugh and pat her on the head. But when Paul stood as though frozen by such questions, Papa looked dreadfully worried and lectured him for hours.

It was unjust. She could lose herself in dreams too.

On an impulse she took her father's arm and held him back while Paul and her mother went on ahead past the police station.

"Papa, listen. When Thasos was called a continent and the Thasians ruled cities in Thrace and had a big navy and trading fleet, Darius told the people they had to sink their warships. Then he made them give a huge feast for Xerxes and his army, and it bankrupted the treasury. And Mr. Kalligas was telling me about another big feast that the people here had to give a Bulgarian garrison during the second world war. And that was only forty years ago. There was a cook in Limena, and he told the fishermen to bring him a catch of dolphins. He cooked them up and served them, and the whole garrison—two hundred eighty soldiers—got violently sick because you can't eat dolphins, Mr. Kalligas said. Then the cook and the people who served the feast had to hide up in the mountains until the war was over."

"That's so impressive, Lily," her father said.

"No, no!" she protested furiously. "Don't talk that way!"

"What way?" he asked mildly.

"It's *not* impressive. It's what happened. But what I wanted to tell you was this. You know that sleepy old man who sits on the bench near the baker's every morning? Well—he was the one who cooked those dolphins!"

"I'm speechless," said her father.

"Not quite," Lily noted tartly.

Mrs. Corey and Paul were down the street near the

butcher's, talking to the handsome policeman. As Lily and her father joined them, she saw the reflected light of a street lamp sparking off the policeman's dark glasses. He wished them all a good dinner, bowed, and went on by. Rosa waddled confidently toward the tables of a taverna where her master, the lawyer, was sitting with friends, all of them nibbling at little bits of dried squid, which they ate with their drinks of ouzo. As usual, the lawyer was wearing his prosperous-looking suit of salt-and-pepper tweed. He stood up and shook hands with all of the Coreys, and Rosa wagged her tail once. Mr. Corey had let Lily taste ouzo; it reminded her of licorice. The Greeks always served it with water. They served water with nearly everything, it was so precious on the island.

Efthymios welcomed them, flicking a napkin at the only table that had an umbrella. They knew he prized it, and although they would have preferred to sit at another table—the umbrella made them feel a bit as though they were in a cave—they felt obliged to accept the honor of sitting beneath it. Still, though the faded canvas flaps drooped down, Lily could watch passersby—the best thing about eating outside on the street.

An old man went past carrying a loaf of bread shaped like a discus; two girls arm-in-arm, laughing, their hair combed up and teased into enormous dark beehives; a plump lady, hurrying, her face peering out from a huge bouquet of roses she was carrying; couples; several families with small children; and an old fisherman in a black sweater, whom Lily and Paul had seen setting out in his caique to fish by himself. Although the fisherman's face was ridged with deep wrinkles, his hair and beard were black.

"Odysseus," Mr. Corey said to Lily.

"Too short," said Paul.

"Too short for what?" asked their mother. "I've seen him stand in his boat and lean on those huge oars, and it looked like he was rowing away the whole Aegean."

People stopped to speak to them, to ask them if they liked their supper. They even made comments about how the fish was fried—too long, said the cobbler—and how thick the soup was—the right way to make it, said a sister of Stella's who lived on the road to Panagia.

They hardly ever spoke about home anymore, Lily observed to herself. When they'd first come to Thasos, they'd compared life here and back in Williamstown. They'd found the house uncomfortable, not having dependable electricity or plumbing or a refrigerator and furniture, and there was not much either, it had seemed at first, to choose from in the markets. She recalled how, on their third day in Athens, before they had come to the island, she and Paul had spotted a dusty box of American cornflakes in a grocery shop window and how they had stood in front of it for what seemed an hour, wishing they could eat it all up.

But they didn't notice the discomfort anymore. When Lily walked into the kitchen and saw the table covered with huge strawberries, or yellow-green zucchini as slender as her fingers, or four pomegranates, blood-red in the sun, she couldn't think of anything that was missing.

"I've been thinking about it, and I don't believe I can

bear seeing that movie again," said Mrs. Corey. "What if, instead, we go to the pastry café and eat cake?"

Everyone agreed to that. Mr. Corey paid Efthymios-Onassis, and they set off for the café on the quay, which was usually crowded all evening with people drinking coffee and eating ices, or cakes made from walnuts inside honey-soaked leaves of pastry so thin they looked transparent, or small, hollowed-out chocolate buns filled with cream, or puddings redolent of oranges and cinnamon and vanilla.

On their way they passed through the main square, which was, Lily thought, like a vast living room for the entire village. Beneath the overarching branches of two enormous plane trees were shops that stayed open until late evening, a tourist restaurant, and several tavernas in which the older men of Limena often came to sit and visit with each other, drinking wine or ouzo very slowly during the hot, still hours after midday. Sometimes a young boy from a nearby coffee shop would pass among the men carrying brass trays with small white cups of Turkish coffee and tall, moisture-beaded glasses of very cold water. Lily, crossing the square of an afternoon, had heard the clicking of the amber-beaded circlets that the men moved rapidly through their fingers—worry-beads, the tourists called them—and that were said to calm a restless mind.

Local people as well as Greeks from the mainland were laughing and gesturing and eating at the tables set out in front of the pastry shop. Next to where the Coreys sat down a whole family watched raptly as a plump little boy about two years old was fed by his mother. After each spoonful of honey cake he crowed like a rooster, and his dark-eyed, black-haired mother would laugh, holding up her head and leaning back so that Lily could see a thin chain of gold closely circling her beautiful, long neck.

"Would you say my neck is long or short, Mom?" Lily asked.

"It's sort of retractable, like a turtle's," said Paul, grinning.

"For someone with an acorn for a nose—" Lily began, then stopped. Paul was looking beyond her shoulder, his expression surprised, then joyful. He stood up and waved. The other Coreys turned to see what he had seen.

"Who's that?" Mr. Corey asked.

"Jack," Paul said somewhat breathlessly. "Mom, he's the American I told you about. He lives in Panagia."

Jack was standing past the last row of tables, his hands in his pockets. He stared at Paul expressionlessly, then gave a curt nod. A dark-haired man had also halted several yards away from Jack and was looking at the Coreys. Paul looked confused as though he didn't know what to do, sit down again or remain standing.

"Maybe they'll have coffee with us, fellow-Americans and all that," said Mr. Corey. He got up and walked toward Jack, Paul following him. Lily noticed that the dark-haired man didn't come forward but stood absolutely still, poised as though on his toes for a leap.

"Where did you meet him?" asked Mrs. Corey.

"Up by the acropolis," Lily answered, keeping her eyes

on her plate. It was odd that when you had something to hide, you were at once sure that someone was looking for it.

Mr. Corey and Paul returned with Jack and his father, and the woman who had served them their desserts brought two more small folding chairs. Jack sat down—reluctantly, it seemed to Lily—next to Paul; his father sat next to Mr. Corey, who asked them what they'd like.

"We won't have anything," the man said in a deep, harsh voice. "We eat much later. I'm Jimmy Hemmings. I gather you know Jack here. Everyone on the island knows us. Strange to meet up with Americans. We thought we were the only ones, didn't we, Jack?"

Jack looked up at the sky wordlessly.

Mr. Hemmings wore a black leather jacket and a black T-shirt. He looked much younger than Mr. Corey. His eyes were a brilliant, piercing blue, and his lashes were as black as his hair.

Mr. Corey explained how and why they'd come to Thasos. Mr. Hemmings nodded rapidly and muttered *uh-huh* constantly, as though hurrying Mr. Corey on with his story.

"A teacher. Well. I've been a teacher too," he said when Mr. Corey stopped talking. "I've taught languages for one thing. I speak several languages, including Magyar—"

"—You mean Hungarian?" Mr. Corey interjected.

"If you prefer," replied Mr. Hemmings somewhat loftily. "We're here mainly for Jack. I wanted him to see a thing or two before he gets too old to appreciate a

foreign country—before prison walls close around the
growing boy—and so forth. Also, I've been doing a bit of
prospecting up in the mountains. There's more than
marble on this island. There're precious metals and ores. I
guess we've been here about eight months, wouldn't you
say, Jack?"

Again the boy said nothing. Mr. Hemmings frowned
for a moment, then went on.

"We had to take care of our residency requirements, of
course, so we went to Istanbul last month."

"We went just across the Yugoslav border to take care
of ours," Mr. Corey said.

"You should have spent some time there; you should
have gone to Skopje, at least, not to mention the Adriatic
coast. Terrible bureaucracy here," Mr. Hemmings continued. "Have you ever tried to have anything sent
through the mail? A chap in Berlin sent me some pipe
tobacco, and the postal taxes were just too expensive. It
was a matter of principle with me not to pay them, so I
left the tobacco in the post office. Let them smoke it—I
wish them joy of it. So you children have met before?
And where was that?"

The two boys were mute. "Up near the acropolis," said
Lily in a low voice.

"Ah, well, Jack goes everywhere. He's damned marvelous! He takes care of himself—the best thing, of course.
Jack's been an independent fellow since he was four,
haven't you?" He stared intently at his son.

"I guess so," muttered Jack.

Mr. Hemmings stood. "We'd best push on. Drop by

and see us in Panagia," he said. Lily didn't listen to what her father said in reply. She was watching Paul and Jack. Paul was whispering something in his ear, and Jack nodded several times and whispered back. Mrs. Corey said, "Goodbye," in a loud voice, the only word she'd spoken since the Hemmingses had sat down.

The Coreys watched them thread their way around tables and disappear among the people on the quay.

"I'm trying to remember what he said," Mrs. Corey remarked in a puzzled voice. " 'Drop by'—what on earth does he mean? I've known people like that man. They tell you everything, you think, then when they've gone, you realize they've told you nothing."

"He lets Jack go anywhere—by himself," Paul said.

Mrs. Corey looked at him reflectively as though he had asked a question. All she said was, "Perhaps Jack doesn't have much choice."

There was a great deal of noise around them, most of it pleasant, animated talking and children laughing, the clatter of cutlery and plates, the soft wash of waves against the quay. But Lily felt a kind of waiting silence at their table. She recalled other such moments when, it seemed to her, each person in her family had drawn away to a secret place. Once it had happened when she and Paul had been shouting and fighting in the back seat of the car, for hours, she guessed, during a summer trip to Maine. Mr. Corey had pulled over to the side of the road. Neither of her parents had turned around. She and Paul had gradually quieted, and they sat there for some time, no one speaking. Another time, her mother had stood up abruptly from the dinner table and gone to the kitchen, from which Lily had heard the sound of a glass breaking. It was right after Granny Corey, who was visiting, had complained that the children's clothes really needed ironing—they looked like laundry sacks, she'd said. After her mother returned, they'd finished supper as though their lives depended on not making a single sound.

This time it must have been something about Mr. Hemmings and Jack that had made everything feel strange, unfamiliar.

But the feeling passed as they strolled along the waterfront toward the small hotel where they had first stayed, where Lily had seen the shepherd leaning on his crook, standing in the middle of his flock of sheep. On their way back Lily ran to a small tourist shop in whose cluttered window a tiny alabaster goat stood on an embroidered wool bag. Every week she asked the price of it, and Mr. Panakos, the owner, would exclaim, "Ah me! It costs the same as it always does," as though the price had nothing to do with him.

Not far from the shop was Giorgi's taverna. As they neared it, Lily heard applause and loud shouts and the music of the bouzouki. Standing at the entrance, looking in, were Mr. Kalligas and Costa, the museum keeper. The Coreys went to speak with them. The two men greeted them all warmly, but their attention returned at once to what was happening inside the taverna.

Tables had been moved back to make a space. In the center of it Mr. Hemmings was dancing, his head thrown back, his eyes closed, his arms raised high like the wings of an angel in flight. Dimitrious, the barber, was sitting in a shadowed corner playing, his head bent over the bouzouki, his hands moving nearly too fast to see.

He had cut Paul's and Mr. Corey's hair several times. Lily had gone along with them to the little triangular shop near the ferry harbor. He often had to put his scissors down and go on a savage fly-killing expedition around the walls. He was a very handsome young man. But when he laughed, you could see he had no teeth left. Mr. Kalligas had explained to Lily that Dimitrious had gone to Kavalla and had all his teeth pulled out because he couldn't afford all the dental work he needed, and he couldn't afford false teeth either. Now and then a tourist would promise to buy him a fine set of teeth if he would go to Berlin or Paris, or some other place with them, and sing in a night-club. Dimitrious was always willing but, Mr. Kalligas reported, the tourists would forget about him and go back to their ships, leaving him and his bouzouki on the wharf.

The music grew louder and seemed about to explode the instrument itself. Jim Hemmings whirled, knelt, kicked out his long legs, sprang up like a great cat, clapped his hands, and snapped his fingers; and though Lily had been troubled back at the pastry shop when the man spoke to her father and ignored her and her mother, she couldn't help but admire him now. The Greeks watching followed his every movement and gesture, their eyes gleaming. She glimpsed Jack Hemmings standing near the barber, his eyes open wide, looking at his father with adoration. Then, gradually, the dance began to grow slow, and the music softened. Mr. Kalligas touched both children on their shoulders, beckoning to them to follow him outside.

Lily especially liked that about Mr. Kalligas, the way he often would take her and Paul aside and speak to them seriously.

"A great, great dancer," he said to them. "Rather an awful chap! Cold as ice! But we all follow him into the sea if he dance like that. What a devil of a dancer! I heard new people coming along here. Did you know that? A Danish man and his family. He comes to draw the Temple of Halyke. You know about that—"

Costa interrupted him with shouted words too fast for Lily to understand. They both grabbed Paul, gripped him with their hands, and lifted him straight up in the air, shaking him like a giant rattle. Costa swiped at his ankle. Lily saw, with horror, an enormous black millipede drop to the ground and scuttle away into the dark. Paul seemed frozen as they set him back on his feet. "What!" he exclaimed, then shuddered. "What *was* that?"

Mr. and Mrs. Corey appeared at Paul's side, bending over him solicitously.

"He's all right," Mr. Kalligas said. "I save him. You got to look out for those things. The bite is badder than the snake." Costa, who was gentle and hardly ever spoke about himself, patted Paul on the back and whispered, "Good, good . . ."

"Did you see it?" Lily asked as they walked home.

"Don't talk about it," Paul said firmly. "I felt it. That was enough."

The music of the bouzouki faded away.

"I think that's enough wildlife for you today," Mr. Corey said to Paul. "Sea nettles, millipedes—what next?"

It was dark along their path except where moonlight scattered silver coins among the pebbles. Lily shivered. She wasn't thinking of the millipede but of Jack. Just as they had left Giorgi's, she had seen him standing outside the circle of men congratulating his father. His eyebrows had been drawn together, and she had noticed his fists, clenched tightly at his sides.

SIX

"CHILDREN, TIME TO get eggs and bread, but, please, no more wildlife," Mrs. Corey called from the kitchen where she and Mr. Corey were drinking their morning coffee.

"You can choose," Lily offered Paul. She was standing in his doorway. He didn't look up. "You get the millipede," she said. He rested his chin on one knee as he tied his shoelaces so tightly his sneakers puckered.

"The laces will break," she said. He shrugged.

"Well, I'll get the eggs then." She lingered a moment, then went off. In the great open space of Poseidon's temple a woman who was hanging up sheets waved and called a greeting to her. By the time she returned home, four brown eggs in her hands, she felt more cheerful.

Paul left the house immediately after they'd finished breakfast. Mr. Corey shouted after him, "Paul! Come back and make your bed!"

He raced back into the house, his jaw clenched. Lily watched him throw the blanket over his rumpled sheets.

"Where are you going?" she asked a little timidly.

"I have things to do," he muttered and ran down the hall and out the gate.

Lily tried to read. After she'd read the same few sentences a dozen times and not gotten them into her head, she wandered into her parents' bedroom. Mr. Corey was very carefully sharpening a short pencil with a kitchen paring knife. She had hoped they could talk together a couple of minutes before he started work, although she didn't have anything much in mind. Mrs. Corey suddenly ran into the room.

"Gil, you pinched my knife! How could you! You have no respect for the grand meals that knife helps me turn out."

"I apologize," Mr. Corey said, grinning and handing over the knife. "I'm simply trying to find things to do so I won't have to write."

"I can help you with that," said her mother. "You can begin with the laundry. First you heat the water."

Neither of them was paying her the least attention. She went back to her room. She wished the goats would run through it again. She was tired of the Persians and the Greeks and their endless warfare. She stared out the window at the mulberry tree. Was that the tortoise lying among its thick roots? Should she go and see? Well, she thought, she'd better get used to mornings without Paul. She was nearly positive he had gone off to meet Jack somewhere. She had hoped they wouldn't meet him again, but they had. That was that. She decided to go to the museum. Maybe Christos or Nichos would be there. Though they were much younger than she and very shy, they were friendly and would talk with her.

The museum stood in a corner of the agora. As she went toward it, Costa called out to her from across a field where broken columns lay partly hidden by tall grass and dog roses. He was holding up a scythe, from the blade of which dangled a snake like a thick brown vine.

He had caught it for her, he said. Everyone in the village knew how scared she was of vipers. Mr. Kalligas, trying not to smile, had told her there was an old man who lived up on the mountain who would cure her if she was bitten. He had a forked stick that he placed so, Kalligas had said, jabbing her arm with two of his fingers, and the poison would be gone at once.

She waved to Costa and told him she was on her way to visit his museum. She walked up the path, past the bird and the huge statue of the youth, and into the cool interior. There were only a few rooms, but they were filled to their ceilings with statues and columns and ancient pots and friezes and tablets. Very little was kept behind glass. She could pick up the shard of an ancient jar and hold it in her hand until it grew warm. She could rest her palm lightly on the heads and shoulders of sculptures of gods that had been made thousands of years ago when people still believed in them.

Artemis and her twin brother, Apollo, were her favorites

among the gods. Apollo was the god of light, she had read. He could be menacing, too, as he looked to be in a small statue of him she had discovered behind a broken stone shield. It seemed all of the gods had contrary natures. They were both marvelous and terrible, like Artemis, who protected young creatures but was also Hecate, goddess of the dark and of the crossways where three roads met, places of evil magic. She was the moon goddess, too.

Lily stood on the tiled floor of the museum, holding a fragment of a small marble bird, recalling a night during their second week on Thasos when she and Paul had waked up at the same hour and met on the balcony. The Aegean had been like a great pale flame stretching to the coast of Macedonia, a black line across the water, and the sky had been filled with a milky light as though there had been a silent explosion of stars. They had never seen moonlight such as that.

As she was leaving the museum, she met Costa holding Nichos by his hand. Costa's skin was faintly pocked. His deep-set brown eyes expressed gentleness and patience. He was not sharp and funny and fast like Mr. Kalligas, but Lily liked him as much as she liked the older man. Costa often helped her father look up words in Mr. Corey's Greek-English pocket dictionary; he seemed charmed by the small green-leather book, holding it carefully in his hands as he looked through its pages. He had learned a few English words from it. He tried out a phrase now.

"How ere you?" he asked.

Nichos giggled and covered his mouth with his hand.

"I am well," Lily replied in English.

Costa grinned and hurried back into Greek. "Good," he said. "Nichos has come to help me with the antiquities. We must move some of those old warriors out of the garden and into the museum." The garden served as extra storage space. Through a window beyond the museum entrance hall Lily could see the old warriors. They were in so many pieces it seemed they must have been fighting for several thousand years.

Costa clasped Nichos to himself for a minute, telling Lily to stay as long as she wished, then led him off to the garden.

The Greeks seemed especially affectionate toward children and, Lily thought, amused by them. Strangers on the streets of Athens had often paused to speak to Lily and Paul, patting their faces and hair tenderly.

She walked down the lane, pausing to watch the baker lift up toward his large oven a wooden paddle upon which reposed eight loaves of unbaked bread. It would be, she guessed, the third batch of the morning.

But not everyone was at work in Limena. Through an opening to the quay between two houses she saw several children astride bicycles. Among them, riding like furies, were Jack and Paul, and trying to keep up with them, laughing and clapping his hands, ran Nichos' little brother, Christos.

With a flourish Jack reversed his bicycle, jumped from it, and raised his hands like a champion prizefighter who has won a bout. Paul was grinning at him and applauding.

Suddenly, Jack grabbed up Christos, roughly set him down on the handlebars, and raced off.

Lily sighed and made her way to the House of the Turk. She hadn't looked in on it for some time. It had belonged to a Turkish official who had lived on Thasos until 1912, when a Greek admiral had freed the island from the Turks and returned it to Greek sovereignty. She and Paul had found the door unlocked and wandered through the empty rooms, on whose stone floors leaves had drifted and piled up. There was a garden in the back of the house with a grape arbor like a roof of leaves. It shut out the sun entirely, and it had been wonderfully cool beneath it.

As she climbed the steps to the door, missing Paul's company, her head down and filled with vague, gloomy thoughts like gray clouds, a voice said in English, "Hello, Miss. I think you are one of the Americans I heard about. Perhaps."

Lily looked up. Standing in the doorway was a tall fair man in a loose white shirt, wearing rope sandals. He was carrying a small round-faced child with a gondolier's hat on the back of her head, its red ribbon hanging straight down.

Yes, she was American, Lily said. A dark-haired, slender woman joined the man and smiled at Lily. "Ho, how pleasant," remarked the man. "We are Danish. We are the Haslevs. Here is Hanne, my wife, and Christine, my daughter, who is not quite two, and we are to live in this house for a time."

"I think I heard about you from Mr. Kalligas," Lily said.

"Oh yes," said Mrs. Haslev. "We met Mr. Kalligas, the ear and eye of Thasos."

"I am an architect," Mr. Haslev said, setting the child down on the step.

"He won a prize," said his wife. "The prize is to be the first to draw a *new* ancient temple, just excavated. It is in Halyke. Have you been there? We are eager to see it."

She had never been there, Lily said. It was on the other side of the island; she had heard you could reach it only by boat. Then she told the Haslevs that she and her family lived not more than a few minutes away.

How had they found furniture for their house? wondered Mr. Haslev. He desperately needed a worktable. There were beds in the house and two very grand if broken chairs, which he could fix. But a table was a problem. "You would like to see the house?" he asked Lily. She nodded quickly, not mentioning that she had seen it before.

"Beautiful!" Mr. Haslev exclaimed suddenly, waving his hands toward the harbor and the sea. He picked up his daughter and they all went inside.

They must have arrived some time yesterday, Lily guessed, but the rooms had been swept clean. In one, there was a small folding bed. "For Christine," said Mr. Haslev. Two mattresses were draped over window sills, airing. The beds themselves were made of woven rope. "Very good," Mr. Haslev said. "Even commodious." They had cleaned and scrubbed out the tile cooking trench in the kitchen, and Lily saw the remains of a breakfast picnic on the floor.

"It is the water closet that puzzles me," said Mr. Haslev. "In fact, it horrifies me," he added, and shuddered. His wife laughed, and the little girl joined in.

"Even my child laughs at me," Mr. Haslev said. "But you come and look."

He crossed the room and flung open a door to a dark, dank closet. There was a large hole in the floor.

"Can you imagine what lives down there? Serpents, I'm sure. Of course, it is impossible as it is. We should all fall in and never be heard from again. I must think very hard about this."

He said he was to start work at the temple very soon; now they must get settled. Lily suggested they all come home with her and meet her parents. They agreed at once. Even though they were so well organized and had, it seemed to Lily, already settled, they were the most care-free people she'd ever met.

Her parents—especially her father—were delighted to have unannounced visitors. It certainly wasn't like home, Lily noted to herself, where people had to make arrangements to visit weeks ahead.

Mrs. Corey made coffee, and they all went to drink it on the balcony.

"It's all so splendid," Mrs. Haslev said, looking out at the sea agleam in the late morning sunlight.

Lily brought crayons and paper and sat down on the floor with Christine. While her parents and the Haslevs exchanged histories and told each other why they had come to Thasos, she drew cats and houses for the little girl.

Mr. Haslev said, "You must come with us to Halyke on the boat. We are to be left there for a week. You can spend the day, and our boatman will bring you back to Limena. I have heard it is beautiful there. And it is so unknown. Hardly anyone has seen the temple except the archaeologists."

"It will probably be a few days," Mrs. Haslev said.

"Anytime," Mr. Corey said quickly.

As they got up to leave, Mrs. Corey asked Lily to go down and find Paul. It was nearly time for lunch.

Lily walked back to the House of the Turk with the Danes. "I think I will find a table somewhere in this village," he said. "Or else I must make one."

"There's Mr. Kalligas," Lily said. "I think he's coming to see you. He'll know where to find a table."

Mr. Kalligas was carrying a white plate covered with a cloth.

"For you," he said, holding out the plate to Mrs. Haslev. "My wife make." He pulled back the cloth, revealing a dozen or so tightly wrapped grape leaves shimmering with olive oil. "It make you bite your fingers," he said. "Inside is the Greek rice, the best."

Lily said good-bye to everyone and ran down to the quay.

Paul was still there, but he had used up his drachmas. He was leaning against a wall watching Jack course about the quay in wide circles, Christos perched on the handlebars.

"He's not supposed to ride kids like that," Lily said.

Paul frowned and turned away from her. Jack was

heading straight toward them, his legs pedaling furiously as Christos roared with excitement. Jack slammed his feet down on the pavement. Christos tumbled off and ran to join a group of children nearby who had been watching enviously. Jack motioned to Paul, staring straight at Lily with no expression at all, as if she'd been a bench. The two boys whispered together. Lily called out, "Mom says you have to come home for lunch."

She saw Paul's shoulders stiffen, heard Jack laugh disdainfully. Then Jack rode away and Paul started up the quay toward home. She ran to catch up with him.

"Will you go to the theater with me this afternoon?" she asked a little breathlessly. "If you don't have anything else to do?"

"I'll think about it," he said. They walked on, saying nothing more to each other even when Rosa waddled down the steps of the police station and came to greet them with her one-swing tail wag.

⌐⌐⌐ Paul didn't go to the theater with Lily that afternoon. Instead, he got a job, work with a cobbler a few afternoons a week. It would be pretty casual, he told his family. Some days the cobbler had no work to do and spent the time in a taverna with his cronies. But on others there could be a pile-up of sandal orders. In an hour or two he had taught Paul how to cut out and staple leather straps to plastic soles.

"How much does he pay you?" Lily asked curiously.

Paul frowned, then shook his head. "I forget," he said.

" 'The laborer is worthy of his hire,' " said Mr. Corey in his quoting voice. "You really ought to know what your wages are, Paul," he added.

"Well—I just can't remember," Paul answered lamely.

Mr. Corey left the kitchen where they were sitting and returned in a moment with a postcard. It was a photograph of a marble statue of Athena. He pointed to her sandals.

"Look how solidly and beautifully they're made," he said. "Progress is all downhill."

"You might as well complain about weather," observed Mrs. Corey.

"If the cobbler made sandals like that, he wouldn't have hired me," Paul said.

"Good point!" exclaimed his mother.

Lily hoped that on his free afternoons Paul would take walks with her the way he had during their first months on Thasos. But he seemed only to want to hang around the house. One day he sat on the balcony for two hours with an opened book on his lap. Lily, leaning over his shoulder, noted that he hadn't turned a page in all of the time he'd been there.

"Where's your friend?" she asked him suddenly. He started as though she'd dropped a ceramic jar on the tiles.

He closed the book and stood up. He took a step toward the doorway where Lily was standing. She didn't move.

"Jack," she said uneasily. "I meant Jack."

Paul sat down in the chair again. Not looking directly at her, he said, "He's working as a deckhand on that little boat that goes to Prinos Beach. There're lots of tourists now. He wants to make money. It's a good job. It leaves him free till the middle of the afternoon."

What do I care? Lily asked herself, sitting in the other chair. But she knew she did care. And she guessed that Paul had found a job because Jack had. It was awful for her to be interested in someone she didn't *want* to be interested in.

She stared at her brother. She hadn't realized how tall he was getting. He wasn't really chubby anymore. His face seemed longer, and his hair, much darker than hers, had begun to curl at its edges. She suddenly recalled how she'd cut his hair when he was around ten and she was eight. She had started, seriously enough, snipping neatly, then cut a great hank of hair. To her surprise, he'd urged her on, both of them giggling in front of a mirror. Then they'd walked into the living room where their parents were sitting. Her mother had stood up and shrieked. Lily started to smile, remembering. Paul glanced at her. He'd been sitting so stiffly. Now he seemed to relax. The book he'd been clutching fell to the floor. He began to talk about Jack.

Jack wanted to be independent, he said, earn his own pocket money so he wouldn't have to ask his father for handouts. He had plans to go to every village on the island. He was like that—he wanted to see everything.

Lily watched his face grow animated. She wanted him to stop talking. At the same time she wanted to know more. How did Jack get back and forth from Panagia? she asked. He couldn't sleep in the acropolis every night.

One of the drivers of the little tourist taxis lived up there, Paul told her, the very short driver who always had a cigarette hanging from his lips. He brought Jack down in the morning and took him up the mountain in the evening.

"I know that driver," she cried. "He has the most beat-up taxi—it smokes like a chimney and snorts like a wild pig!"

"But it's a free ride," Paul said triumphantly.

There was a secret argument going on between them. Lily knew she wanted Paul to stop caring about Jack. Paul told her, in one way or another, that he wasn't going to stop.

⎍⎍⎍ "Please, Paul, take away that bone," said Mrs. Corey who was about to flip over a large Spanish omelet she was making for supper.

"It's so old," Paul murmured. The bone was smooth and dark like a piece of polished mahogany. He held it against his own arm. Yesterday, on the way to their swimming place off the rocks, they had seen a Greek they knew working in the agora. All of the sites in and around Limena were now filled with French people and the local men they had hired. As the Coreys were passing by, the Greek, a waiter at Giorgi's taverna in the evenings, had shouted a greeting at Paul and tossed him the bone. The archaeologist in charge had said Paul could keep it— they'd found many skeletal remains and they could spare one radial, as he called the bone. It was probably one thousand years old, he had told Mrs. Corey, who could speak a little French. When they returned home after their swim, Lily had drawn a picture of a person with a forearm missing, floating over the agora in ghostly robes. She'd smiled at her drawing, but when she'd gone to Paul's room to show it to him, he'd hardly glanced at it. She saw the bone lying on his bed. "Aren't you going to add it to our collection?" she'd asked him. "You can have all that stuff," he'd replied indifferently. "I'll probably give this to Jack. He'll like it."

Lily had walked out of his room without a word. Her mouth trembled and her face had felt fevered. In the hall, she stared down at the basket in which she and Paul had saved all the things they'd found since they'd come to Thasos, bits of jars and corroded coins they had dug from piles of earth in various places around the agora. She had wanted to cry out to Paul that he could give the whole collection to Jack for all she cared.

But she did care. They had had such good times digging out those relics, too broken or too small to be of much interest to the archaeologists, but things that had conjured up a lost time for Lily and Paul.

"Lily! You look like you're trying to set the table in midair," said Mrs. Corey. Lily started and put the plate she had been gripping down on the table.

"Paul," Mr. Corey said sternly, "that is definitely not a kitchen bone. Now please, do as your mother asked. Take it somewhere else."

As Paul passed Lily on his way out of the kitchen, she muttered, "I thought you were giving it to Jack."

"He didn't want it," Paul replied mildly. "He's only interested in coins."

She placed a fork next to the plate, then went to the door. Paul was squatting next to the basket. She saw how carefully he placed the radial bone in it. She felt a touch of shame. When he walked back toward the kitchen, he gave her a vague smile as though he hadn't suspected she had meant to taunt him with her question.

"Come along," Mrs. Corey said. "The omelet is hot, and we must eat supper and get to bed early."

In the morning, before the heat of the day began, they were to meet the Haslevs at the harbor. The fisherman whom Mr. Corey called Odysseus was to take them to Halyke in his boat. But there was a large blot on the day to come for Lily. Paul had invited Jack along, and he was coming.

"Why does he have to?" Lily asked her mother when they were alone.

"Lily! I thought you'd given up whining!" Mrs. Corey exclaimed.

Lily was silent, staring at the floor.

"You must try not to resent him," her mother said more gently. "He doesn't have much of a home, I think."

She suspected her mother didn't like Jack any more than she did. As if aware of her thought, Mrs. Corey said, "Liking isn't the last word."

The Haslevs were already on the quay the next morning when the Coreys arrived, boxes and straw baskets and canvas bags piled up around them. Christine sat in a little canvas chair wearing her gondolier's hat, waving a wooden spoon as though conducting an orchestra. Everybody else wore hats, too—you had to. By midday the sky would be white with heat.

On the water below them bobbed a large crescent-shaped boat. Kneeling in the middle of it was the boatman, tinkering with a kerosene engine. "He does look like Odysseus," Lily murmured to her father. The soles of his leathery bare feet were dark as eggplant. From time to time he grabbed up a handful of greasy-looking rags and wiped his fingers, never lessening his concentration on his engine. Mr. Haslev saluted the Coreys by holding high a bottle of Thasian wine.

"I think I forgot needle and thread," Hanne Haslev said.

Mr. Corey set down two picnic baskets. One held small bottles of carbonated lemonade and water. The other held the picnic Mr. and Mrs. Corey had made that morning: two loaves of crusty bread, hard-boiled eggs, tomatoes, cucumbers, feta cheese wrapped in damp cloths, fruit and a cake they had bought the evening before at the pastry shop that would be fresh still because it had been soaked in orange juice. "That alone will make our journey worthwhile," said Mr. Haslev as he peered into the basket. "And with a new temple thrown in."

It took some time to load the boat with everything the Haslevs needed for a week: sleeping bags and boxes of food and supplies. Then, as though the drama of the occasion were not enough, Odysseus stepped on the blade of a knife buried among the rags and cut his heel. He reached under his black sweater, fumbled in a pocket,

and took out a package of cigarettes. With a long finger-
nail he slit open one of the cigarettes, then emptied the
grains of tobacco into the wound. Mrs. Corey gasped.
The boatman shook his head at her, smiling. "It's good,"
he said. "Good. It will sterilize the wound."

The boatman had told Lily and Christine to sit midway
between bow and stern. Lily's feet rested on one of a pair
of enormous oars fit for a Titan.

"But we can't go yet," Paul said urgently. "Jack isn't
here."

She had forgotten all about Jack. For a moment she
hoped he wouldn't turn up, or that they would leave
without him. He was late after all. Why shouldn't they
leave? But then she glimpsed him sauntering toward the
boat along the quay as though he had all the time in the
world. As he drew close, Lily noted that despite his cool
demeanor his shoulders were rigid, his arms held tightly
against his sides. Bits of straw and grass clung to his shirt
and pants. He must have slept in some dark hole last
night, in the acropolis or a shepherd's shelter in the hills,
she guessed.

Each time she saw him, she would be disgusted by his
arrogant ways. But then she would see something—like
the straw and grass, or a long tear in his clothes, or his
fingers, the nails so torn it was as though he'd gnawed
at them in a fit—and she would feel the reluctant pity
that had struck her that night in the shack on the beach.

Jack jumped down into the boat and squeezed next to
Paul on a seat in the bow. Paul whispered to him, looked
quickly at his mother, who was staring out to sea, and

reached into the picnic basket. He took a peach and handed it to Jack, who looked at it rather critically for a moment, then took a very small bite. Oh, why didn't he gobble it down if he was hungry, Lily thought.

It was nearly seven o'clock when Odysseus stood up and shoved the boat away from the quay with one of the oars. The village by then was stirring with life. Shutters were flung open at the windows of the whitewashed houses; people had appeared in the square and opened their shops to the day. Here and there among the leaves of trees were spots of vivid color, red and orange and purple, the petals of flowers in pots and window boxes. The hill above their house rose like a great green wave, and Lily saw the apron of the theater and, more distant, the dark fortification of the acropolis.

Christine was singing in a piping voice like a bird. The kerosene engine thumped into life, and the old sailor stood up as they passed through the harbor entrance. He looked, thought Lily, as though over the years he had grown a hard, salty skin that could endure the ravages of storm and sea.

For the first hour Lily spotted familiar landmarks, the old wall, the rocks where they swam, then the beach with the shack. She glanced at Paul and Jack as they passed the beach. They were grinning and talking as they looked at the shore. How dumb boys are! How could they ever grow up to become men like Mr. Haslev or her father, or Mr. Kalligas and Odysseus?

Now the hills were much steeper, there was no sign of the great wall anymore, but still Lily could see small terraces far up their slopes where old olive trees grew. Nearly two hours after they'd left Limena, Odysseus brought the boat closer to the island. They were chugging toward a narrow, tapering peninsula. Scattered along it were huge sections of marble columns.

Mr. Haslev, shouting above the noise of the engine, told them some war party must have landed on the peninsula thousands of years earlier. The Greeks, who had quarried the marble from the hills, had fled, leaving their unfinished work behind them. Lily, looking straight up, her straw hat falling off, thought, it is the same sky they looked at. Everything else has changed but that.

They rounded the peninsula and came into a harbor where the water was as clear as glass, revealing large, flat, light-brown stones lying on the bottom, across which darted schools of tiny silver fish like filaments of wire. Odysseus turned off the engine, and they drifted toward shore. On the pebbled beach stood three whitewashed huts with blue-painted doors. They appeared deserted. But then, from a small stand of pine trees, an elderly couple emerged, hurrying past the houses toward the hill on the other side. The woman carried the same kind of wooden paddle Lily had seen the baker use, and in fact, there was a round loaf of bread on it. Odysseus said they were shepherds. "They run away from people—they only like their animals," he said. In October, he told them, there would be a few more people, who would come to harvest the olives growing high above them on the hill.

The old couple disappeared as the bow of the boat ground over the pebbles onto the shore. A great sunny silence hung over them. Everyone sat unmoving for a moment. Then Odysseus stepped out onto land. Lily observed that the cut on his foot had closed up.

They all helped carry the supplies up the beach to a larger hut, farther back from the shore than the others, that they had not seen from the boat.

"But where is the temple?" Lily asked Mr. Haslev.

"We will soon see," he answered. "But first the duty things."

Mr. Corey, carrying a box of Swiss canned meat and tea and sugar, suddenly put down the box.

"Paul! Jack!" he shouted.

The two boys had gone to one of the huts, and Paul was watching Jack as he flung himself again and again at the blue door.

"What is the *matter* with that boy?" Lily heard her father say to her mother. Paul had turned to look at Mr. Corey, but Jack continued to strike the door with his hands and his shoulders. Then Odysseus shouted something of which Lily could make out only the word *no*, and Jack stopped. He stood for a moment looking at the door, then walked to where they were standing, his face sullen. Paul trailed behind.

"That house belongs to someone," Mr. Corey said sternly.

"I just wanted to look inside," Jack said, kicking pebbles, his shoulders hunched.

"You can look inside our house," Mr. Haslev said, smiling. Jack didn't respond, only continued to kick at the pebbles.

Everyone except Paul and Jack crowded into the hut. The walls were thick. Small windows let in light that fell on the hard-packed earthen floor. Odysseus set down a basket he had carried in and went outside to lean against a wall and smoke a cigarette. The hut was bone-clean except for mouse droppings trailing through the tiny cavelike rooms.

Mr. Haslev swept away the droppings. Directed by Hanne, they put away supplies. Christine had set her canvas chair in the center of the largest room and was sitting on it, dreamily watching people move around her. Lily took the lemonade and water bottles down to the water and propped them up with stones. The small waves lapped gently at her hands. When she looked up, she glimpsed Jack and Paul moving among the pine trees.

The Haslevs and the Coreys had emerged from the hut, Christine straddling her father's shoulders. "Now we shall go and see the old, new temple," Mr. Haslev said. "Actually," he added, "it's only a part of it—the portico."

Thirty yards or so behind the hut stood a line of willow-like trees. As they approached them, Jack and Paul suddenly appeared in front of them.

"We saw it," Jack said. "It's little." He looked at Paul as though for confirmation. "It's very little," he repeated and suddenly barked with laughter, as though, Lily thought, they were all fools to be there.

Mr. Haslev looked disconcerted for a moment. Then he said firmly, "It doesn't matter at all how large or small it is." Everyone moved on past the line of trees.

The portico stood before them in an open space, the

ground covered with stones. Its slender columns were a pale apricot color, and through them Lily saw the blue sea.

"There's nothing between us and Turkey," observed Hanne.

"This is the most faraway place I've ever been," said Mrs. Corey.

They spoke softly as though not to wake something, or someone, who might be sleeping inside the portico.

"There are graves nearby," Mr. Haslev told them, almost in a whisper, "and cult shrines." Christine lowered her head until it rested on her father's.

Suddenly, Jack emitted a loud war whoop. Christine started and grabbed her father's forehead, and Lily jumped a foot from where she'd been standing. Paul was laughing silently a few yards away. When Lily glared at him, he stared back at her stonily. Everyone appeared to be making an effort not to look at Jack, but Lily shot a glance at him. He was grinning uneasily, off by himself near the trees. As she turned her head, she glimpsed Paul walking quickly to stand beside him.

"Are there snakes here?" Lily asked her mother. She felt frightened all at once. The beautiful small temple seemed a fading dream. She stared at the ground.

"You know they're pretty much everywhere," Mrs. Corey replied. "You also know they don't go after people. Why don't you have a swim? I'll walk to the beach with you. Pretty soon, we can have our picnic."

By the time Lily had stripped to her bathing suit, she heard the boys shouting in the water. She saw Paul leap up and try to duck Jack. They gripped each other's shoulders and sank out of sight for a few seconds, emerging smoothly and swiftly like two dolphins, to laugh and shake their heads, drops of water flying around them.

Lily sat on her towel, and her mother sat down next to her.

Lily sensed her mother's gaze on her. She felt a strange kind of embarrassment. After a moment Mrs. Corey put an arm around her. "You may feel like a wallflower, Lily," she said, "but you look like a beach flower to me."

Lily leaned against her for a moment.

"What does Jack want to do that for—mess up everything?" she asked as she stared at the boys who were swimming now toward the peninsula, close beside each other, their brown shoulders shining, and sleek as seals.

"I can think of a reason or two. I don't know they'd explain much," Mrs. Corey replied. "You know, if we were at home and Paul met a boy like Jack, there would be other friends who would"—she hesitated—"who would interest him too. But here, there's only Jack."

"What about me?" Lily burst out. "Aren't I enough?"

"And they're different, Jack and his father," Mrs. Corey went on, as though she hadn't heard Lily, "and mysterious." Then she began to pin up Lily's braid, taking the hairpins from her Greek bag that was embroidered with yellow stars and green crosses. "Oh, Lily," she mumbled, a pin in her mouth. "It isn't that at all! You're enough—you're plenty!"

Lily didn't think so.

Her mother said, "No person can be *everything* for another person."

Lily got up, ran to the water, and plunged in. As she swam underwater for a few feet, she opened her eyes and saw, dimly, the round stones on the bottom. They looked like watery loaves of brown bread. She burst through the surface and faced down the small harbor, toward the sea, toward Turkey. For some time she was able to forget all about Jack.

SEVEN

MR. HASLEV's drawings of the portico of Halyke were spread out on the long table he had found, with Mr. Kalligas' help, and which he had set up beneath the thick branches of the grape arbor in the garden. He had let Lily look at them as often as she wished since the family had returned to Limena, explaining to her each addition and change he made in the elevations.

He had improved the terrible water closet, reducing the size of the gaping hole and painting the walls white. The Haslevs had scavenged about in tiny hill villages, finding odd bits of furnishings the Greek owners were glad to sell to them.

Now they had plenty of chairs, two small tables, and even a small, intricately carved chest of drawers. They were beautiful, Hanne said. But the villagers didn't want them anymore. They wanted new plastic furniture. It was all very well, she told Lily, for foreigners like themselves to admire the lovely old stuff, but for the people of Thasos that stuff meant being poor, not having all of the things they imagined the rest of the world had.

The two families often ate supper together. The Haslevs partly made up to Lily for Jack's intrusion into the Coreys' life.

Paul spent nearly every waking hour with Jack. Since his work at the cobbler's was very casual, he was able, now and then, to go with Jack on the pleasure boat to Prinos.

Sometimes Jim Hemmings appeared at twilight in the square beneath the plane trees, his motorcycle slowing down, snorting like a halting bull, the noise breaking into the sweet murmur of early evening. Then he would ride Jack home to Panagia. But often as not Jack stayed with the Coreys, sleeping on an old mattress Stella loaned them. He spoke to Mr. and Mrs. Corey in monosyllables, always moving restlessly, making a struggle not to chew away at his fingernails, Lily saw. But at least he spoke.

On those nights he stayed Lily could hear the mumble of Paul's and Jack's voices late into the night. One time she crept from her room to Paul's feeling ashamed and frightened lest they catch her there outside the door. She held her breath and listened. Inside the room they grew silent.

One morning Mr. Corey went with Lily to get the breakfast eggs. He told her a little about the book he was writing, about the thousands of children, led by Peter the Hermit on a crusade, who'd been abandoned in Marseille, lost, or sold into slavery. On their way back through the temple of Poseidon he suddenly said, "One of Jack's troubles is—he doesn't want to let his father know he *isn't* marvelous, that he's just a boy."

A friendly goat was nuzzling Lily's hand. It must be easier to be a goat than a human, Lily thought, except you could end up as somebody's dinner.

That morning they were to go to Kavalla. Mr. Corey needed to visit the American library there to find a reference book. Paul had pleaded to stay. When his parents remained adamant, he had reproached them, saying they were always talking about discipline and doing your work. How come they were ready to take him away from it just to go to a library? When he had finished at the cobbler's, he was pretty sure he could go and stay at Mr. Kalligas' house until they came home. Paul had loved going to Kavalla last time. Now, Lily knew, he didn't want to miss a day with Jack.

Paul was not Jack's only follower. Manolis, Paul's Greek friend, spent any time he could be spared by his father from the making of the terra-cotta jars, down on the quay with other children who had come to watch Jack ride a bicycle. Just as his father excelled at dancing, so Jack had become the champion rider.

At midday, usually, the children would begin to gather near Giorgi's taverna. Jack would appear, swaggering, his pocket full of drachmas he had earned on the boat to Prinos. He could bring the bicycle's front wheel up sharply, balancing on the rear wheel. He rode in intricate fast circles so close to the edge of the quay that he appeared to be hovering over the water. He would finish his performance by sailing down the embankment above the streets of the ancient city, his hands held high above his head. The boys who could pay for the bikes would try to copy his exploits, but caution held them back. The smaller boys would ask Jack to give them rides, especially little Christos, whose voice would rise in a wild cry of delight when Jack lifted him to the handlebars.

Lily grew bored with herself for always saying to Paul that Jack was not supposed to ride the children like that. He paid no attention to her anyhow. When she told him she had asked Mr. Kalligas about the village beneath the sea and he had said there was no such thing, Paul only shrugged. "It wasn't a lie," he said. "You hear all sorts of stories in a foreign country."

He sulked all the way to Kavalla, staying on the narrow deck of the *Maria* and glaring at the water. From the wharf in Kavalla, where vendors sold everything from head scarves to plaster replicas of Venus de Milo, you could look up narrow cobbled streets to the acropolis and a Byzantine castle and beyond them to the great aqueduct striding across the hills. It had been built by Suleiman the Magnificent in the 16th century. Kavalla was bright and lively and full of people, and Paul began to look more cheerful, more like his old self.

After they went to the library, they ate in a big, airy restaurant where Lily had a large plate of buttery mashed potatoes, her favorite food. Mr. and Mrs. Corey had several errands to do. The children wandered back to the waterfront and walked around the old market, which was just up the hill above where the *Maria* was anchored. "For you, a very special price," said an old peddler to Lily when she picked up a small brass pot. She pulled out the pockets of her slacks to show they were empty. The old man laughed, picked out a plum from a small heap of fruit, and handed it to her. "Then you must have this for comfort," he said.

"There's Mohammed Ali on his horse," Paul said, looking down at the wharf. The equestrian statue towered above the crowds of people moving about the wharf. Mohammed Ali had once ruled Thasos. Now birds perched on his head.

"I'm glad we're going home soon," Paul said suddenly.

She could feel the meanness in her coil to strike like a snake. But she restrained herself and didn't ask him how he could bear to think of leaving Jack Hemmings.

They went back to Limena in the late afternoon. There were two white goats tethered on the deck of the *Maria*, and they bleated mournfully all the way to the island. The cabin was full of people crowded on long wooden benches. Among them was Mr. Spyros who owned the movie theater. One of these days, he promised the Coreys, he would get a new film to show. By that time everyone in Thasos—except the nuns from the convent in Theologos—would have seen the film he was now showing, and that was only just, didn't they agree?

As they walked home, Mr. Xenophon emerged from his store to ask them how their day in Kavalla had been. Mr. Kalligas, who must have spotted them from his house as they trudged up the slope, came out to remind them of the fair in Panagia next week. Lily had forgotten about it. Mr. Corey said he was eager to go. "I'm so glad we'll see a real island fair and get to Panagia. More to remember."

But Lily wasn't so eager. She was sure that Mr. Hemmings would be there, honking and boasting, dancing and kicking up his heels.

They went to Efthymios-Onassis for supper. Afterward, in the warm dark beneath a sky full of stars, they started for home. Dimitrious stepped out of the shadows near the museum and, playing the bouzouki softly, walked with them all the way, whispering good night to them at their gate.

It had been a fine day, a day without Jack. But tomorrow he would be back. When he wasn't showing off his bicycle tricks, he would be pulling leaves from shrubs, jumping at the lean stray cats that skulked in alleys, his hands and feet always moving. Even Rosa waddled away at a fast clip when Jack was in her vicinity.

Lily had seen him once on the deck of the Prinos boat. He had paced ceaselessly, fiddling with ropes, kicking at the railing. He was like an engine racing, with no place to go.

⎍⎍⎍ The sun-washed island, its meadows and slopes and mountains, grew gray and black and seemed to shrink beneath the violent rain that swept across it on the day of the Panagia fair. Cloud formations like a monstrous sky fleet turned black over Limena. A wind blew up, howling as it passed among the trees. The sea boiled and foamed.

Shutters banged against walls. The house felt entirely different, like a cave smelling of damp stone and earth. Open stands and carts were quickly dragged inside beneath flapping canvas awnings that strained at their ropes. The rain beat down until Lily, looking out at the balcony, thought she was seeing the village under water that Jack had told them about.

Toward late afternoon the rain slackened. There was a long crack in the dark sky, and light poured through it like a ray from a lamp in the night. An intense scent of earth and plants rose from the garden and flooded the house with a green smell that was both rank and sweet. The sun struck the yard and the mulberry tree with points of light like the tips of arrows on fire. Gradually, the sky cleared and turned blue.

The storm brought the island the first good rain since the Coreys had been in Thasos. The wells would be full now, Lily knew, and the narrow streams in the mountains would become torrents that would overflow their banks.

The Coreys and the Haslevs were going to the fair together in two of the little taxis. Mr. Kalligas was to ride with them. He had told Lily the day before that he was especially glad to be going because, along with the fair there would be an engagement party for his great friend, Grigoris, and Juliana, the girl he was to marry.

Lily had run into Mr. Kalligas at the baker's where he had just taken a joint of lamb to be roasted. He had told her about Grigoris. He had been in a serious accident on a fishing boat that crippled him so severely that he could get around now only on crutches. He was rich, Mr. Kalligas said. He owned three boats in the fishing fleet that set out every evening from the quay. And he had loved Juliana since he was a boy no older than Paul. But her parents did not want her to marry a crippled man.

"Every night for one week Grigoris put his crutches against Juliana's house and sit down on the road. And every night Juliana's mother and father look out and see him sitting there. All night long, and in the morning when they get up, he is still there. Seven days he do this."

"How did he get up without his crutches?" asked Lily.

"What you think! Juliana's mother go out and help him up. She get to know him very, very well.".

"But she knew him before, didn't she?"

"All his life, since he was a baby. But not this way. She did not know how stubborn—like a donkey—he is. He told her he's going to sit in front of her house for a year—until she say okay."

"Why didn't they want Juliana to marry him?"

"Stupid!" exclaimed Mr. Kalligas, looking down toward the water. "But she give in. I will introduce you. You will see! Grigoris is handsome, my God! Like a god! But his poor legs . . ." Abruptly, he stopped talking, and his face grew stern as he peered down at the quay.

"Look at that boy! With Christos on that machine! I tell him and tell him not to do that. I must speak to Costa," he said.

Lily, looking in the same direction, saw, as she expected, Christos riding the handlebars of a bicycle Jack was turning in ever-narrowing circles. Mr. Kalligas left, walking with his quick, neat steps toward the museum. How could Costa prevent Christos from chasing after Jack?

The Coreys had a light supper—Mr. Kalligas had told them there would be wonderful things to eat at the fair—and went to pick up the Haslevs and Mr. Kalligas. They all walked down to the quay and piled into two taxis.

On the long muddy climb up the mountain they passed a roadside shrine that Lily had gone into one afternoon when she was roaming around by herself, when Paul was off somewhere with Jack.

Inside it she had found a small altar in front of which stood a rickety table crowded with thin, honey-colored candles in tin holders. From the walls and the altar hung tiny silver replicas of legs and arms and eyes. Mr. Corey, when she described them to him, explained to her that people who were blind or who had diseased limbs left the replicas there in the hope of miraculous cures. Was it possible that among them hung two little silver legs left by Grigoris? She thought not. From what Mr. Kalligas had told her, Grigoris sounded as though he didn't need miracles.

The road leveled out along a high ridge above the coastal valley far below, and beneath the starry sky the waters of the Aegean glowed like banked embers.

If it had not been for the stars, they could hardly have made out the streets and houses of Panagia. It was so dark—dark as the world had once been, Lily thought, until the coming of electricity. But after they had left the taxis and begun to walk, she observed a yellow glow that, as they drew closer to the village center, she saw was made up of lanterns suspended by cords above long oilcloth-covered tables. There was a burst of noise, of laughter and talking. Groups of people moved about the cobbled streets dressed in their best clothes, some carrying babies, others, surrounded by small, excited children.

A powerful smell of rosemary-scented lamb, grilled on open fires, hung over the village like a cloud. Lily saw dishes of pickled octopus, stuffed vine leaves called *dolmades*, pans of moussaka, dishes of cucumber and yogurt, and *tryopitakia*, pastries filled with cheese. Everywhere reposed large platters of peaches and melons and pears.

They drifted through the thronged streets, parting only to meet again before a table of rugs and blankets woven by the village women, or one sagging with the weight of brass pots and pans hammered out by the men, and they would frequently run into Mr. Kalligas who knew everybody and wanted to introduce them to everybody.

Lily could hear the bubbling rush of a stream that tumbled down the mountain and sped through the village in a narrow channel. The cries and talk of the fairgoers would rise and fall. In a brief lull Lily heard the whirr of cicadas like tiny motors inside the velvet dark that lay at the edges of the village, biding its time, she thought, until it overtook it like a besieging army.

They all met up with each other in the village square, and Lily saw Dimitrious there, playing his bouzouki. A circle of men were dancing, snapping their fingers in the air. Gradually they dropped away until there was only Jim Hemmings in his black leather jacket, his blue eyes like periwinkles, piercing in the amber light of the many lanterns strung around the square. People clapped and cried out as he stamped and circled and leaped—electricity jumping through the dark, Lily thought. He paused in front of a table where a handsome young man sat, a pair of crutches leaning against an empty chair. Then, his arms raised high, he began to pirouette, clapping. A dark-haired, rather plain young woman was sitting beside the young man, and with them were four older people.

"That's Grigoris," Mr. Kalligas said to her, poking her arm.

Mr. Hemmings danced in place, his eyes always on Grigoris. Was he honoring him? Lily wondered. Or was he showing him what it is to have strong, healthy legs?

Far on the other side of the square, near the entrance to a small hotel, Lily saw Paul standing with Jack, his arm around the taller boy's shoulders. Like everyone else's, their eyes were glued on Mr. Hemmings, who suddenly seized a glass of wine from Grigoris' table and downed it without ceasing to dance. Then he swiftly knelt at Grigoris' feet. The bouzouki music ceased abruptly. Grigoris grabbed up one of his crutches and tapped Mr. Hemmings on his back as though knighting him.

The crowd melted away until the square was empty except for a few people sitting at tables. Mr. Kalligas took the Coreys and the Haslevs to meet Grigoris. Jack and Paul, Lily saw, were no longer in front of the hotel.

Grigoris turned to Lily and smiled and shook her hand.

His betrothed smiled too, revealing a small gold tooth that flashed like a golden needle. Were they enjoying themselves? he asked. And did they like Thasos? He had a strong, calm voice. It was easy to imagine him sitting stubbornly on a road for seven days, for a year if that was what it took to win his bride. Lily guessed that the older woman sitting next to him with a puzzled expression on her face must be the bride's mother, still surprised that Grigoris had made her give in to him.

Mr. Hemmings, who had ducked briefly into a small taverna next to the hotel, reappeared, waving two bottles of wine, and Grigoris asked everyone to sit down and talk a while and take a glass of retsina. The Coreys and the Haslevs both said it was time they left for Limena. Mr. Kalligas told them he would find a way home; he wanted to visit with Grigoris for a while.

"Here! Do stay," Jim Hemmings said to Mr. Corey. "Don't go running off in the night when the party is just starting!" His words were slurred. As he sat down, he knocked over a chair next to him. He kicked at it and laughed foolishly.

"Thanks. I have work to do and must get up early. And the children must get to bed," Mr. Corey said.

"Oh yes, the children . . . and professors and their work," Mr. Hemmings muttered. Then, as though they had already left, he turned to Grigoris and took one of his hands in his own. Looking at his face for a moment, Lily saw it soften. It was surprising to think Mr. Hemmings might really like someone.

On their way back to the taxis they paused at a table

laden with food. Behind it stood the man who had sold Mr. Haslev his worktable, and they greeted each other like old friends. He urged them all to try the sweets his wife had made only that morning.

"Where is Paul?" asked Mrs. Corey suddenly as Lily downed a piece of honey cake.

"Somewhere around," Mr. Corey said. "He'll turn up."

"You better go look for him, Gil," said Mrs. Corey in an uneasy voice. "Lily! You look so sleepy!"

"It's because I'm stuffed," Lily replied.

Mr. Corey had taken only a few steps back toward the village center when Paul and Jack appeared, their faces two pale ovals in the dim light.

"Can Jack come home with us?" Paul asked his father.

"I don't know if there'd be room in the taxi," Mr. Corey said. But Mrs. Corey said quickly, "We can manage. Lily will sit on my lap."

It was an uncomfortable ride down the mountain for Lily. Each time they went over a bump, she bounced up and her head hit the roof. I'll have a flat head, she told herself, all because of Jack.

The taxis let them off at the quay. Compared to Panagia, Limena seemed as lit up as a big town. As they walked toward home, Jack and Paul ran ahead until they disappeared from view. Mr. Haslev, carrying the sleeping Christine, began to whistle.

It was a lonely, sweet tune. They passed Mr. Xenophon's, and Lily saw the dim glow of a lamp on a table like a distant campfire, illuminating the faces of several men drinking coffee and brandy.

"That's so beautiful," Mrs. Corey said when Mr. Haslev had ceased whistling. "Is it a Danish folk song?"

Mr. Haslev laughed. "No, no. It's a song by Sidney Bechet, the great American saxophonist. It's called *Petit Fleur*."

⎍⎍⎍ Lily lay in her bed, her eyes heavy with sleepiness as she looked out her window to the sky. She tried to hum *Petit Fleur*. It was like a little silver bird flashing in the woods; it vanished when you tried to fix it with your eyes.

She believed that if she could memorize it, every time she sang it she would be able to bring back the mysterious feeling of the fair, the glowing campfires of Panagia and of Mr. Xenophon's table of friends, the black mountain forest between them, the bursting energy of people like a small intense light in the dark.

Her mother came into her room, holding the tiny flashlight she always kept by the side of her bed in case the electricity failed.

"It was amazing up there, wasn't it?" she asked Lily, tucking the quilt around her.

"Yes, it was amazing."

"Will you remember it all, Lily, when we're back home?"

"I'll always remember," Lily responded, waking up a bit. "I just wish I could get that tune Mr. Haslev whistled." She hesitated, then asked, "Why did *he* have to come home with us? He was already home in Panagia."

Her mother didn't answer for a moment. Then she spoke carefully the way, Lily knew, grown-ups do when they don't wish to speak directly about a thing.

"I believe Jack didn't want to stay with his father—"

"—because he was drunk," Lily stated.

The flashlight went out.

"Yes," Mrs. Corey said.

EIGHT

LILY AND HER MOTHER were standing next to the wisteria, looking out at the path, which had undergone a striking change. For days the village masons had been working on it. Now there was a long flight of new broad stone steps leading all the way up the hill to the theater, where that night a company of the Greek National Theater was to give a performance of *Iphigenia in Aulis*, written by Euripides more than two thousand years ago.

But the transformation of the path had an awful consequence for Stella's ancient relative. She was crouched on the ground in front of her house, weeping. Stella knelt beside her, trying to comfort her.

"Why can't she crawl across the steps just the way she did over the little stones?" Lily asked, so distressed she was clutching her mother's skirt just as she remembered doing when she was little. "It's only about six feet. That hasn't changed."

"But it was her entire world," said Mrs. Corey. "You know she's nearly blind. The path to the water tap was a journey for her, but she knew every inch of it."

Stella rocked the old woman in her arms. Lily tried to imagine herself on the edge of a deep chasm where there had once been a bridge. For a second she was sure she felt the dread that must be gripping the woman.

"Why is it you can really imagine how it is to be someone else, then you forget—all in a second?" Lily wondered.

"It's a kind of gift," her mother said. "It comes and goes."

Stella was lifting up her great-great-grandmother and slowly pulling her toward the tap. When they reached it, Stella turned on the water. The old woman reached out a hand, felt the thin stream of water, and a smile appeared on her faded lips. She extended one foot, then the other, to wash them, Stella murmuring to her all the while. When she had finished, she started the crawl back across the steps. Mrs. Corey and Lily stood there, watching, until the two women disappeared into their yard.

"Only one week and a half before we go," Lily said.

"Ten days," said Mrs. Corey. "And in two weeks we'll be home. The leaves will have started to turn."

⌐_⌐_⌐ "It won't be like going to a play at home," Mr. Corey said to Lily. "It's more like going to church."

The Coreys, except for Paul, were drinking coffee in their kitchen with the Haslevs. Mr. Kalligas had found a baby-sitter for Christine, a young cousin of his, probably the only person in Limena who would not see the play. Paul and Jack had been hired for the evening by Mr. Xenophon to sell lemon and orange drinks to the audience before the play began.

"We shall go in a procession—in the ancient way," said Mr. Haslev. They had all been aware of the people streaming past the Coreys' gate for the last half hour. They were unusually quiet. As the Coreys and Haslevs joined them, they found themselves on a step behind Mr. and Mrs. Kalligas. Mr. Kalligas whispered to Lily, "The play begin at sundown when the parliamentary member arrives. But, you will see, he will be late."

Lily had once seen the deputy who represented Thasos at Athens, driving to the ferry in his big black car. He was a short old man with a head of beautiful white hair. He lived outside of Limena in a big house near the village olive press.

When they stepped onto the apron of the stage, most of the marble benches that rose up the side of the hill were filled. Lily sat down next to her mother on a bench from which she could glimpse the roof of their house. She rested her hand on the warm, twisted trunk of an ilex tree. The sun was slowly sinking, leaving behind it a great rose blush on the horizon. Jack and Paul moved about on the stage, shouting up at people as they brandished small bottles of fruit-flavored soda. Far out on the water the fleet had begun the night's fishing. The boats looked like fireflies. Among the audience Lily saw the familiar faces of the butcher; the grocer, Mr. Xenophon; the owners of the shops and restaurants, which would be closed during the performance; the baker; the cobbler; even Odysseus, the sailor.

People suddenly murmured and shifted about in their seats. The deputy and his wife arrived, and the deputy bowed and waved to the crowd as they walked importantly and slowly to the bench that had been reserved for them down near the stage. As soon as he sat, Lily heard the slow, steady beat of a drum. But suddenly the two tall spotlights on either side of the stage blinked and went out. People responded with subdued merriment, clapping softly and laughing. In a minute or two the lights flickered and came on. The drum, which had stopped when the lights went out, began again, louder now and faster. And when the beats were coming so fast that it sounded like one booming echo, they suddenly ceased utterly; and as though he'd sprung out of the earth, Agamemnon stood in the center of the stage.

The commander of the Greek armies, whose ships lay becalmed in the gulf of Aulis, looked enormous. His breastplate glittered. Lily saw he was wearing a mask. He began to speak. Though Lily could not understand classical Greek, every note of his voice sent shivers up her spine.

Mr. Corey had told her the story of the play. A hare, an animal loved by the goddess Artemis, had been slain with all its young by the Greeks. To appease the goddess and ensure a safe voyage to Troy for his ships, Agamemnon was told he must sacrifice his eldest daughter, Iphigenia.

The lights of the fishing fleet had vanished. The audience seemed to hold its breath as the tragedy of Iphigenia marched like the beat of the drum toward its end. Masked women in long costumes of gray cloth recited the final words, which Mr. Corey had read to Lily in English that afternoon. She recalled only the last lines:

> *Beloved light*
> *Farewell!*

There was no applause at first, and then it thundered out, filling the bowl of the theater. People rose and made their way along the edge of the stage. The actors had disappeared behind two huge rocks. Lily wondered if they would look smaller in ordinary clothes.

The Haslevs stopped at the Coreys' for a visit. Lily brought a kitchen chair to the balcony to sit with them. Her mind was dazed with images of the play; she hardly listened to the conversation among the adults until her mother wondered aloud where Paul had gone.

"I saw him with his friend sitting on the wooden crates of soda near the steps. They went away before the play ended," said Mrs. Haslev.

"They had to take the crates back to Xenophon's store, probably," said Mr. Corey.

It was not Paul who appeared at the entrance to the balcony a few minutes later, but Mr. Kalligas. He stood, mute, in the light from the hall. One by one the Haslevs and the Coreys turned to him, smiling.

"I have a bad thing to tell you," he said.

"What?" Mrs. Corey cried out. "What is it?"

"Not your son," Mr. Kalligas said. "Not the son of the dancer. It is Christos. He fall from the bicycle."

Mrs. Haslev groaned. "He's hurt?" she asked.

"He is dead," Mr. Kalligas said almost inaudibly.

Her mother rose and clutched Lily to her, holding her hands against Lily's ears as though to stop her hearing what she had already heard. Lily pulled at her mother's wrists until her hands fell away. There was the sound of running feet in the hall. Everyone was standing, looking past Mr. Kalligas. Paul stood there. He looked up at his father and began to sob. They leaned forward staring at him, listening so intently that his sobs could have been words, telling them what had happened.

He brushed at his face with a fist, gave a shuddering sigh, and began to speak in a forlorn voice, like someone who knows there can be no comfort against the misery he feels. "We went down to the bicycles. Some of the kids met us. The bicycle man wasn't there—"

"Everyone was at the theater," Mr. Kalligas interrupted sternly.

"—And we rode around the quay for a while," Paul went on. He stared at Lily and repeated what he'd said as if in that way he might postpone what he must tell them.

"Paul. Tell us," his mother pleaded.

"I am!" he cried out.

"All right . . . all right . . . calm down," muttered Mr. Corey. Paul looked at his father as though he'd said something unbelievable. "Jack and I gave the little kids rides," he said. "Then Jack took Christos. He went on the embankment path. I saw the bicycle skid. Jack fell. The bike, with Christos on it, went over the side."

"The doctor come but he can't do nothing," Mr. Kalligas told them.

"It was dark," Paul said. "Jack rides better than anyone. But it was so dark . . ."

"Do the parents know?" asked Mr. Corey.

"Nichos went to get them."

"I want to go home," Hanne Haslev said. Mr. Haslev took her arm, and they went down the hall and out the door. Mr. Kalligas stayed on, following the Coreys into the kitchen, where Mr. Corey began to wash up some coffee cups. Paul went to stand by the table, pressing one hand down on its surface and staring at his fingers spread out like a starfish. Mrs. Corey moved distractedly about as though in search of some object. She turned abruptly and stared at Paul. "Go and wash your face," she said shortly.

Mr. Corey shook out the cloth with which he'd dried a cup and hung it carefully from the lip of the sink. What a fussy thing to do, Lily thought.

"Go where?" Paul asked in a bewildered voice. "We wash up here—in the kitchen."

Mrs. Corey gave a nervous, quick laugh. "Yes . . . yes. You're right. I forgot."

"You were warned, Paul," Mr. Corey said grimly. "You were told it was dangerous to ride anyone on the handlebars."

"Boys do dangerous things," Mr. Kalligas declared. "My own son, too. He nearly fell off the acropolis. Now he is grown and works at his job in Germany and doesn't do no more dangerous stuff."

"Where is Jack?" Lily asked. They all turned to look at her. She wondered if they were as startled by her voice as she was. She hadn't spoken since before the play began. So much had happened after the first beat of the drum that had separated day from night. In the play there had been a death that had taken place out of the sight of the spectators. Another, real death had happened down the hill from the theater. Her thoughts ran wildly in all directions, and most of them were questions she didn't believe anyone could answer.

"That boy—he run away," Mr. Kalligas said.

"Does his father know?" wondered Mrs. Corey.

"I think he is in Thessaloniki. That's what he tell Giorgi yesterday—that he must go there."

"How terrible!" exclaimed Mrs. Corey. "Jack will be frightened, alone."

"Not that one," declared Mr. Kalligas.

Jack had stayed with the Coreys the last two nights. Since he didn't speak about his father unless it was to boast about him, nobody in the family ever knew where his father was.

"The police will want to talk to him," Mr. Kalligas said. Paul flinched and timidly asked, "Why?"

"Because the police always have to ask questions when an accident happens. Also, they like to make everything their business," Mr. Kalligas replied.

"How do you know he ran away?" Lily asked. "Maybe he's somewhere in Limena."

"I know," Mr. Kalligas said. "I hear shouting. Mrs. Kalligas say to me, go see what has happened. I walk down to the quay and I see Jack—running—running—on the Panagia road. I called out, 'Hey!' but he didn't look, just run on."

"Paul?" questioned Mr. Corey.

"The last I saw him," he answered dully, "was when the doctor was sliding down the bank to where Christos was. He just disappeared."

Mrs. Corey, her eyes filling with tears, said, "Those poor people . . . the mother and father . . ."

Mr. Kalligas shook his head. "This is a terrible night," he said. "For Costa, his children are like two little birds." He made a sheltering gesture with one of his hands over the other.

"Could he have gone back to Panagia?" Mr. Corey directed his question to his son. Paul shook his head. "He never stays where they live if his father's away. He told me his father had gone to Salonika." Paul hesitated a moment, then said in a rush, "It's to get a check from a lawyer there. Jack's mother sends them a check every six weeks. She's rich—and all they have to do is stay away from her. That's the deal, Jack's father said."

Lily saw her parents exchange glances.

Paul was looking up at Mr. Kalligas. "Will they *do* something to Jack?"

"What you mean?" Mr. Kalligas asked. "Who? The police? Costa? No, no. The boys been riding like that before you came, even before Jack came. The police warn them. They don't do nothing. And the man who rents the bicycles—he's lazy and greedy. He knows he shouldn't let them. He knows he should get new bicycles. But he takes the drachmas and he drinks the retsina and he doesn't think about it anymore."

Was it one person's fault? Lily asked her mother when Mrs. Corey came in to say good night to her.

"It's everyone's fault, I guess," Mrs. Corey said. "The police who didn't really make them stop, the bicycle man, Jack, Paul, all except little Christos. He was too little to understand the danger—maybe I mean he was too little to *believe* in the danger."

"But if all the others understood, why did they do what they did?"

"Understanding can be fitful," Mrs. Corey said. But her voice sounded uncertain, and even by the dim glow of the shadeless floor light Lily could see how troubled she looked.

When Lily walked into the kitchen the next morning, her mother was asking her father to let Paul sleep. "He was awake during the night," Mrs. Corey said. "I found him in here and asked if he wanted to talk. He only shook his head. He feels very bad."

Lily had heard Paul, too. She had been lying awake, imagining Jack alone somewhere, in the acropolis or among a grove of olive trees.

"I'll get the bread and eggs," she said. Her parents were sitting at the table looking intently at each other. They seemed not to have heard her.

"Could he get into serious trouble?" Mrs. Corey asked.

"I don't think so," Mr. Corey said. "People tolerated

all that wild riding around on the bikes. Of course, that will end now. You could say Jack was being generous, giving a little kid a ride who couldn't afford to rent his own bicycle."

"You could," Mrs. Corey said. "But I don't think anyone will."

"I walked over a railroad bridge over the Susquehanna when I was a kid," Mr. Corey said. "My parents would have gone mad if they'd seen me, stepping on railroad ties, the river rampaging below. The other kids thought I was a star. I could have killed myself . . . or caused some terrible accident."

"And his father always away," Mrs. Corey said, "leaving him alone. He's never said a word to us about all the nights Jack's stayed with us."

"Mom! I'm going to get breakfast," Lily said loudly. They stared at her in surprise as though they hadn't known she was there in the room with them.

The village lay quiet, sun-struck, and the whirring and clicking of insects seemed unusually loud to Lily. Perhaps she could hear them so clearly because there were so few people about. She met Mrs. Kalligas walking down the slope. She was carrying a covered plate.

"The poor little family," she said to Lily. "I'm going there now to take some food. My husband has been there all night."

"Can I go with you?" Lily asked impulsively.

"Oh, yes," Mrs. Kalligas responded. "They'll be glad if you come."

How, wondered Lily, could Costa and his family be glad of anything?

It was certainly true, she observed, as they walked through the village square, that there were far fewer people around than she had ever seen in the morning. When she mentioned it to Mrs. Kalligas, she told Lily that it was because people were so unhappy about the death of Christos, and that many men and women and their children were visiting Costa's house, taking food to the family and sitting with them to comfort them.

Mrs. Kalligas led Lily down a lane where a small group of people were gathered in front of a house and were speaking softly among themselves. Lily saw Stella and Mr. Kalligas. Walking slowly away from them was the village priest, whom Lily frequently saw hurrying down a street. He was called the *pappas*. He wore a long black habit and a tall round hat that was like a stovepipe. His thick beard curled like a bramble bush, a long silver cross hung from his waist, and his dark eyes seemed to bore through people to something inside only he knew about.

The door to the house was open. A ray of sunlight struck the stone floor at the entrance. The rest of a long narrow room was dark. When Lily followed Mrs. Kalligas inside, she saw a row of people sitting on benches along the wall. At the very back Costa and Nichos were sitting on either side of a small, plump woman whose hair was loose and disheveled. Without making a sound she moved her head constantly, her hair swirling about her white face. The three of them looked very small, like

children. They were huddled together as though to protect themselves as best they could against a bitter cold
wind. From one of the women on the benches came a
low, steady sound of weeping. Mrs. Kalligas put down
her plate on a table loaded with other dishes covered in
mesh or cloth to keep the flies off.

Lily stood in the middle of the room. No one spoke
to her. After a moment she went back to the street where
Mr. Kalligas was talking to Stella. Stella looked down at
Lily. She reached out and very gently tugged Lily's
braid, then walked into the house.

"You are well this morning?" Mr. Kalligas asked Lily
as they went back up the lane. Lily nodded. "A dreadful
day, yesterday," he said. "I've been at Costa's all night.
Now that Mrs. Kalligas is there, I can go home." He
paused. "Your brother came, they were glad. Costa embraced him."

"Do people stay all the time?"

"Oh, yes. When there is a death, no one is left alone.
They will stay until the time Costa can go back to his
work. He is too weak now. He can't do anything. He
can't walk."

She and Mr. Kalligas were speaking in Greek. He had
always until that moment spoken English with her. She
hadn't realized it until she had thought, how well he
speaks! Of course, it was his own language! He was a
different man in Greek, not comical at all.

"Do you think Jack went home to Panagia when he
ran away?" she asked.

"Perhaps. This morning early, on the first boat from

Keramoti, I saw his father when I stepped out from Costa's to get some coffee. I ran to tell him about Christos. But he was already on his motorcycle and riding to the mountain like a devil. It doesn't matter. Someone will tell him along the way or when he gets there. The island knows now." Mr. Kalligas paused and looked up at the mountain. "The island knows," he repeated.

After they had parted, Lily went to buy a loaf of bread at the baker's. She held it up to her nose. It had such a cheerful, hopeful smell. For a moment she forgot all that had happened since Mr. Kalligas had appeared on the balcony the night before.

"I went to Costa's house," she told her parents who were still sitting at the kitchen table, much as she had left them. They hadn't even known she was gone! She put the loaf on the table. "I skipped the eggs," she said. Her mother touched the bread, then stood and embraced Lily. "I'm glad you're back," she said. At that moment Mr. Haslev walked into the kitchen carrying Christine on his shoulders.

"Tell us about Costa," Mr. Corey said. There was something new in his voice, as there had been in Mr. Kalligas' voice when he spoke to her in Greek. Her father had asked her the question the way he would have asked a grown-up.

She told them how it had been—the warm, dark cave, the woman weeping, the little family almost hidden in the shadowed corner of the room. Mr. Kalligas had seen Mr. Hemmings earlier, so at least he was back from wherever he'd been. Paul walked into the kitchen while she was speaking. Christine laughed and shouted his name. Paul reached out and wiggled her foot in its worn red sandal.

"If Jack knows his father is back, he'll go home, unless he's already there," Mrs. Corey said.

"There'd be no reason for him to go home," Paul said.

"But if his father—" began Mrs. Corey.

"There'd be no reason," Paul repeated firmly.

⌐⌐⌐ The afternoon dragged along. Through the hot, sticky hours Lily and Paul played silent games of cards, so distracted they would forget whose turn it was to deal. They both made mistakes, which neither of them made comments about. Mr. Corey slowly packed his books and papers. Mrs. Corey, saying they'd have to eat supper no matter what, and she'd have to shop for it but was too tired at the moment to think about it, went to lie down on her bed.

Around six Lily heard footsteps in the hall. She and Paul went quickly to her door. Mr. and Mrs. Corey were across the way. Mr. Hemmings, leaning forward on his toes, was standing there. He looked at each one of them in turn, his heavy eyebrows drawn together over his eyes.

"Is Jack here?" he asked abruptly.

"No," replied Mr. Corey curtly. "We haven't seen him since last evening."

"You?" Mr. Hemmings asked Paul. Paul shook his head.

"If he comes here, we'll let you know," Mrs. Corey said softly.

Mr. Hemmings didn't look at her. Deliberately, it seemed to Lily, he spoke only to her father. "Naturally, he'll come home to me when he's good and ready," he said. "And he knows this island better than many of the people who live here. He couldn't possibly get lost—not if he tried." He turned from them and gazed back to the front door as though to measure carefully the distance between it and where he stood.

He suddenly shrugged his shoulders as though in response to some question he had asked himself. He turned back to the Coreys.

"They tell me," he began, "that Jack was the one who was riding the little boy on his handlebars. I find that hard to believe. He's much too bright to do such a stupid thing. He was flying up and down hills when kids his age were still on tricycles. The Greeks are bound to lie to protect their own. It's natural. After all, we're foreigners." Suddenly, he began to pace up and down the hall as though he were thinking. But Lily didn't think he was. It was more as if he were on the brink of dancing, his steps rhythmic, his body so lithe as he moved.

He turned to them again, keeping his distance from them. "He's a free and independent kid," he said then in a hard voice. "I've made it my business to see that he's that way."

"He's not free and independent if he can't make choices about how he behaves," Mr. Corey said in a voice as hard as Mr. Hemmings's.

"Anyone can have an accident," Mrs. Corey said, taking a step toward Mr. Hemmings.

"I saw him," Paul said thinly.

Mr. Hemmings lowered his head, looking up from under his brows at Paul.

"How could you have seen him? It was dark," he said gruffly.

"He lifted Christos onto the handlebars," Paul said, his voice rising. "And they rode off. There was the crash of the bike hitting the ground. Jack screamed."

"He didn't," Mr. Hemmings contradicted. "He never screams!"

"He did!" Paul cried out. "It wasn't completely dark. There were lights in the fishermen's houses. The bike skidded. I saw the front wheel turn quick. It went over. Jack got himself off. One of his legs was up in the air a second. Then he was standing and Christos and the bike went over the edge—"

He broke off and glanced at his father. Mr. Corey was silent. "He didn't do it on purpose," Paul said. "He couldn't help it."

Mr. Hemmings covered his face with his hands.

"He must be scared," Mrs. Corey said. "But he'll come home eventually."

"Jack is never scared," Mr. Hemmings avowed, but for the first time his voice wavered. He looked at Mr. Corey. "He *can* make choices," he said, but he spoke without conviction now. It almost sounded as if he were pleading for someone to agree with him.

"Paul will help you find him," Mr. Corey said.

"I know some places he might be," Paul said eagerly.

"He sleeps in the acropolis—well, he used to, before he started coming here."

"And at the beach in the shack," Lily offered. Paul looked at her, startled.

Mr. Hemmings stood flat on his feet, unmoving, his shoulders slumped over. "I know he does that," he said sorrowfully. "All right, then. It'll be dark very soon. We'll look for him at first light. We'd never find him now. I have to go see the museum fellow." He stared at them all. Lily wondered if he hoped someone would tell him he didn't have to go to see Costa and his family. When no one spoke, he said, "Yes. I'll go there first."

"Shall I meet you somewhere in the morning?" Paul asked him.

He nodded. "I'll stay at Giorgi's," he said. "He'll put me up."

But it was Lily who found Jack.

NINE

LILY HAD NOT slept a wink. She lay on her bed staring at the open window. It was like a small stage where first Agamemnon leaped into view, his painted warrior's mask shining like the hard face of a huge, angry doll, then Mr. Hemmings, his face masked by his large hands. That afternoon, when he'd taken his hands away from his face, it had looked different, not so much softened as shapeless, his skin full of folds and pouches as though a screw at the back of his neck had been loosened by his worry.

Sometime during those hours she had crept into her parents' bedroom. Next to their bed, on the floor, was a small clock with a luminous dial, which showed her it was just after two a.m. She listened to their even breathing. One of them sighed, but she couldn't have said whether it was her father or her mother.

For a few minutes she sat on the balcony. Beneath a

full moon the sea seemed to quiver. There was no wind. Her bare feet and legs were as pale as marble. She knew she was postponing what she had—at some moment— determined to do. In the kitchen she ate one of the English biscuits they had bought in Kavalla. She went to look in the sink to see if there were slugs curled in a heap around the drain. If she could look straight at them, it might give her courage. But there was nothing in the sink except a peach pit someone had forgotten to throw away.

Then she got dressed. She tied a sweater around her shoulders and wrapped up two peaches and a few biscuits in a cotton scarf. She tiptoed down the hall, out the door and through the gate, and made her way down to the village on the new stone steps.

The moonlit lanes and streets were ashen. The village slept. She kept her eyes away from the shrines, the gates and temples, the old abodes of the gods whom she did not wish to imagine; she was afraid to think about their faintly smiling, inhuman faces, the deep, distant look of their eyes. She thought instead of Paul, his arm reaching up to rest on Jack's stiff shoulders, and the older boy turning to him, bending to whisper something in his ear.

It was a long walk. She tried not to think, not yet. It was her feet that carried her through those moments when she wanted to turn back, go home, draw the cover over her head.

She had left the sea at home—now she had reached it again. Here it made a sound, a soft hissing as the waves uncurled on the sand. In front of the dark shack the oilcloth-covered tables gleamed as though pools of water lay on them. She went past them into the kitchen. A faint smell of fried potatoes lingered in the air. There was no one there.

Lily walked back to the beach. Her heart sank. She had been so sure Jack would be there, huddled on the floor asleep, that her mouth had opened to whisper him awake.

She looked out at the Aegean. Past the beach, the lawyer's house, beyond a point of land, was Halyke. Beyond that, to the east were Turkey and Russia, India and China and Japan, the Pacific Ocean, Australia, the western coast of the United States, the Atlantic, England and Europe, Athens, and back to the spot where she was standing. The vast world! She felt as little as Christine, alone in the center of it.

From the corner of her eye she saw a point of brightness, then it was gone. She gazed at the tiny islet. A light flared up, then another. Someone was lighting matches there in the black fuzz of scraggly pines on the islet's crest. She had once dog-paddled around it, gripping the rocks, and found a narrow path that wound up through the trees. She had not taken it, only looked, wondering about it, kicking to keep afloat.

The light flickered, died. What if it was not Jack but a stranger who had made a refuge of the island? But she was as sure it was Jack as she was that she was standing on the beach, her sneakers filling up with sand. She could imagine how it had been, how he'd run away after the accident, how he'd recalled the shack as a place he could shelter in. He might have spent the day in a dark corner of the acropolis or in the cool depths of the olive-pressing plant, which would be empty at this time of year. Then, at nightfall, he'd made his way here, to the beach. He would have gone to the shack at first, then recalled that *someone* had left him bread and honey. He'd seen the island and gone out to it, not thinking about the next day, only wanting to hide after the terrible event.

Lily took off her sneakers, tied them around her neck, and rolled up her slacks. Holding the scarf above her head, she waded into the water. It was not cold. The sand scrunched delicately between her toes. She hoped no crab would pinch her feet. She was no Spartan who could keep her mouth shut tight. No, she would shriek and run for shore, and Rosa would come barking, then the lawyer!

She had to swim the last few yards. He might hear her in the still night, but that couldn't be helped. He might think she was a dolphin—if he ever thought about such things as dolphins.

She felt her way along the rocks and came to the path. She pulled herself up, gripping the scarf, now soaked, in one hand, and made her way up the pine needle–strewn path. In a small clearing a fire of twigs was now burning, and hunkered down beside it, holding out a stick with a heel of bread stuck on the end of it, was Jack.

Lily squatted down, her clothes squishing with water.

"I figured it would be you," Jack said quietly. He looked at her as he slowly turned the bread. "Last time— I figured it was you who left the bread and honey."

She was too surprised to speak. That he'd ever thought about her at all was hard for her to believe.

"Everyone is looking for you," she said. "I mean they will be in the morning. Your father, Paul . . ."

"And the police, I guess," he said.

"No. I don't think so. Unless you got lost for good."

"I'm not lost," he said defiantly, taking the bread off the stick. He blew on it, then wolfed it down, making a face as though it pained him. He must be awfully hungry.

She unwrapped the scarf. "I brought this," she said, holding out a damp peach to him. He looked at it for a moment, then back at the fire. There was a crumb on his lip from the bread. He was handsome, she saw for the first time. His eyes and brows were much like his father's, and he had the same fierce look. But his chin was different, softer. He took the peach from her, without looking, and put it somewhere behind him. He moved restlessly and began to pluck at the root of a pine tree as though he wanted to tear it from the ground.

"You can stay with us tonight," she said. "In the morning you can go to your father."

He wasn't listening to her. "It happened so fast," he said in a low, brooding voice. "There must have been something slippery on the embankment. The bike went right out of my hands. I tried to catch him. Christos. But his leg was caught somehow. He was lying all crumpled down below. I went and hid in one of the places they've excavated until I saw the people come and get him. I knew he was dead. The men were all talking. They didn't know how to lift him up. His father came."

He let out a sudden gasp as though someone had struck him a terrible blow across his back. For a second Lily thought he would fall into the fire. Then he reared back.

"I wish—" he began. He shut his mouth tightly. Then he seemed to feel the crumb because he brushed at his lips again and again.

She wanted to say, it isn't your fault. But she couldn't say that. He had been the cause of the accident. There was no way around that.

"God! God!" he exclaimed.

Oh—he *was* lost! Had she come to find him to win a prize for finding a lost boy? She couldn't think why she had come. She didn't know what to do. She felt her sodden clothes on her skin and shivered. It would be hard going back into the water, then starting the long walk home. And what was she to say to him?

"Why did you come looking for me?" he burst out.

She answered without thinking. "Because I was sorry for you," she said. Then, because that wasn't all of the truth, she added, "At least, that was one of the reasons."

He jumped back from the fire as though it had grown too hot. "I don't want anyone to feel sorry for me," he said flatly.

"I can't help it," she said.

He laughed at that. It was a clear, free laugh as though something in him had eased. "Okay," he said. "If you can't help it . . ."

He began to put handfuls of earth on the fire. She saw how carefully he smothered it, making sure there wasn't an ember left.

"Don't you want the peach?" she asked. "I brought two, but the other is mushy and the biscuits are all wet."

He searched for the peach among the leaves, found it and began to eat it as they stood there, the fire dead now, a breeze stirring the pines. When he'd finished, he bent and dug a hole with his hand, pushed the peach pit into it and covered it up. "Not enough soil here," he said. "But maybe it will grow."

They scrambled down the path to the water and slipped into it. Lily's clothes weighed on her, and she was relieved to feel the sand beneath her feet. Silently they walked along the road until they came to the crossroads at the stone farmhouse.

"Well—I go up there," he said, pointing at the mountain.

"But you can stay with us," she protested, then remembered. "Your father didn't go to Panagia. He said he was staying at Giorgi's."

He seemed to hesitate, still facing the mountain road.

"He's going to see Costa tomorrow," Lily said, feeling a current of fear, remembering everything at once as though the last half hour of swimming and walking had been time out of trouble.

"I have to go, too," Jack said. "Maybe Christos' father will kill me."

"He won't," Lily said quickly. "Nobody will kill you. Paul went. Costa hugged him."

"He won't hug *me*," Jack said in a cold voice. Lily thought, what if they did do something to Jack?

"But I'm going there," he said. "I'll go to Giorgi's now."

They began to walk toward the village. She could imagine Jack walking into Costa's house, head down, his hands in his pockets, scared and determined not to show it. But it was hard to imagine Mr. Hemmings going even though he had said he would. People like Mr. Hemmings, Lily was thinking, if they ever said they were sorry for one single thing, they'd have to be sorry for their whole lives.

She would have liked to ask Jack why his mother paid his father to stay away, to keep *him* away from her. She would have liked to know everything about his life. She had the feeling that all she would ever know was what she knew at that moment.

They parted in front of the museum. A ray of moonlight fell on the face of the stone youth who had been gazing out to sea ever since he'd been dug up out of the ground.

She started toward home.

"Thanks," Jack said in a low voice after her, "for the peach."

TEN

"YOGURTI! YOGURTI!" cried the boy, banging the wooden box strapped to his handlebars as he cycled slowly down the street. It was startling to realize that in less than a week, Lily might be in the supermarket in Williamstown and she would stop to choose one of the small cups of yogurt displayed on a shelf. She could imagine herself opening it in the kitchen at home, the refrigerator humming, then taking a spoon from a drawer and eating the yogurt, which would be stiff and cold, not like the soft custard of Limena, and she would be staring at the big basket of kitchen gadgets her mother kept on the counter, gadgets she had loved to play with when she was little.

She had been sent to Mr. Xenophon to buy the last can of Swiss milk they would probably need. She lingered by his little table beneath the baobob tree, thinking about what had happened there the night before.

The Coreys had supper at Efthymios-Onassis'. "I've come to the end of what I know how to do with eggplant," Mrs. Corey had said. "So I guess it is time we were going home."

As they left the restaurant and walked down the street, it seemed to Lily that more people than ever spoke to them—strolling families, men in tavernas, people who called out greetings from their gardens. She had wondered if she would ever again live in a village where every single person knew her name.

As they went past the grocery, Costa had called out to them. Her parents had halted, standing motionless as though turned to stone. Costa was sitting at Mr. Xenophon's table, a tall glass of water and a small glass of brandy before him. He stood up and bowed formally to them. All at once, both Mr. and Mrs. Corey had rushed to him and put their arms around him.

It had been eight days since Christos had been buried. Lily felt tears spring to her eyes. She kept her head down. In his low, courteous voice Costa called her name twice as though she were running away from him. She looked up at him, conscious of the tears on her cheeks. He was smiling. He had grown so thin that his shoulders looked like bones without flesh. The pockmarks on his face were like the pale craters on the moon. His eyes had sunk deep into their sockets. But his shirt was neat and ironed, and the hand with which he touched her head was firm and warm. There was hardly any conversation. He asked them if they were well; he'd heard they were to leave Limena very soon. Neither Mr. nor Mrs. Corey asked him how he was. That would have been a cruel and meaningless question, her mother had said later. They only murmured and held his arms briefly, and then they went on home.

As she glanced at the table where their meeting had taken place, Lily felt as though she had already left Thasos, that she was recalling an event from a great distance away.

She walked on, thinking now of home, of her room in the old house in Williamstown. She was going to change it, give away the stuffed animals she had had for as long as she could remember and take down the frilled green curtains from the windows so that the light could shine through, moonlight and sunlight and the gray light of rain.

Paul was sitting beneath the mulberry tree when she came through the gates, reading an English detective story they had gotten in Kavalla. He must have read it ten times by now, Lily thought. He looked up at her, lifted his hand, and bent his fingers slightly. Not much of a wave. He didn't smile, didn't shout some familiar insult at her. He hadn't done anything like that for some time. It wasn't that he had grown silent—he talked to her, and they played cards together—it was more that he had become quiet. He took walks by himself in the village, stopping to visit his former employer, the cobbler, or walking down to the quay to watch the fishermen mending their nets. Lily had followed him several times. She hadn't tried to keep hidden. He had seen her, but he seemed not to have minded.

She knew he hadn't seen Jack or Mr. Hemmings. As far as she knew, no one in Limena had seen them.

Mr. Kalligas had told Lily about Jack's going to Costa's house the morning after she had discovered him on the islet. He had gone with his father. But Mr. Hemmings had not gone in; he had waited outside in the street.

"That boy, he stood in the doorway," Mr. Kalligas reported. "Costa got up from the chair and brought him to the table with the food. He wouldn't eat nothing. Then Nichos run to him and lean against him. I see the boy's face. He looked wild! Pretty soon he left Costa's house. Then he went up to Panagia with his father. They been staying in their rooms. The father go out to buy food. No more dancing."

"Here's the milk," Lily said, putting the can down on the kitchen table. Her father, who was drinking coffee and staring out the window at Paul, asked, "Did your brother speak to you?"

"He waved," she replied.

"I'm always telling him to think," Mr. Corey said, "and now that he seems to be thinking, it worries me." He sighed and put his arm around Lily. "Well, we'll be home soon. Paul will put all of this behind him."

Lily didn't say it, but she didn't think that would happen. How could she and Paul recall only the joyful days? How could there be light without the dark?

⎍⎍⎍ Mr. Kalligas visited the Coreys in the afternoon. As usual, he was bringing news. A huge German company had sent representatives and products—kitchen equipment, all electric—to Limena. They had arrived on the early boat from Kavalla, and that evening the products were to be exhibited in Mr. Panakos' shop. Mr. Panakos had cleared away all of his goods to make room for these extraordinary objects, and everyone in the village would be going there to see how they worked.

"This isn't electric, but it works on batteries," said Mr. Corey, holding out to Mr. Kalligas their transistor radio. "We would like you to have this."

Mr. Kalligas clapped his hands together once. "Bloody wonderful!" he exclaimed. Lily knew he had always admired the radio. He was so plainly delighted that she felt delighted herself. He would take it home to play for Mrs. Kalligas, he said, and then he would come back. He had a gift for Lily.

When he returned a half hour later, he wasn't carrying anything Lily could see. He stood in front of her, smiling, gradually opening his hand. A small piece of terra-cotta lay on his palm. He held it up to the light from the kitchen window. Lily saw it was a carving of a woman's head. Her nose was arrowy, her forehead noble, and her bound and braided hair was so beautiful that Lily gasped.

"Artemis," said Mr. Kalligas. "I give it to you because you like our old gods so much. You see—her ear is missing and a piece of her chin. But she is still there. I found her in my garden. I was planting a tree, digging, digging, and there she was!"

Lily held the little carving in her hand. It seemed to grow warm. Mr. Kalligas was watching her. "I see you like," he said, grinning. She could only nod.

In her room she examined the head. Artemis-Hecate,

goddess of the crossroads. She thought of the crossroads that she had passed six times at night. She thought of Jack and herself on the islet when he had put out the last ember of the fire. She thought of the silence and the darkness through which they swam to the beach.

"Lily," called her mother. "Put on your dress. We're going to the Haslevs for supper."

"It doesn't fit anymore," Lily called back.

"Just don't breathe deeply," her mother said, coming to the door and grinning.

After they had eaten beneath the thick green arbor from which grapes now hung as they hung over the face of the satyr at the Silenus Gate, the two families went for their last stroll together.

"I've never seen so many people on the streets," commented Hanne Haslev.

"It's because of the German exhibit," said Mr. Corey.

"Let's go see," Mr. Haslev said.

There were lines in front of Mr. Panakos' store. Lily peeped through the window. The alabaster goat and the wool bags were gone. In their place were machines, beaters and knife sharpeners and can openers, all whirring and circling madly as people looked at them with intent curiosity.

"How strange," Mr. Haslev remarked as they went on to the pastry shop where they were to have dessert. "Many of the houses have no electricity. Yet the people were so eager . . . did you see how they looked at those things and touched them?"

"They'll all get electricity. They have to. And everything will change," said Mr. Corey, adding pensively, "because it has to."

The next morning, which was the day before the Coreys were to leave, Paul and Lily and their father went down to the village to find some young man they could hire to help them get their bags to the wharf. It would be simple to pack; there weren't any cupboards and chests of drawers to empty. As they went by the museum, Costa came out and called to them. He would like to give Mr. Corey a coffee, he said, and the children something sweet to drink.

Costa led them through the small rooms of the museum across stone floors smelling of damp stone. Costa had been cleaning, as he did every day. Lily saw a dented pail of water standing beside a great terra-cotta bowl. A few yards beyond the back entrance was a cleared space raised a few feet above the meadow, which had been one of the ancient city's squares. The earth was packed down there; sections of columns lay against each other, but several were standing and the right height to serve as chairs. Behind the space ran a tangled hedge. Costa clapped his hands loudly. At once, like a good witch in a fairy tale, an elderly woman dressed in black poked her head up over the hedge. Costa spoke quickly to her, and she reappeared in a few moments with a tray; on it were two cups of Turkish coffee and for Paul and Lily tall glasses of water in which floated strips of vanilla.

Mr. Corey took his Greek-English dictionary from a pocket and pressed it into Costa's hands. Costa's pale skin flushed. He opened the small pages at random, spoke a few Greek words, flushed again as he tried to pronounce their English equivalents.

It was quiet there, the sounds of the village muffled. The two men spoke haltingly to each other. Conversation, though, seemed unimportant. There was a kind of tenderness between her father and Costa that Lily felt directly, just as she felt the warmth of the morning sun.

Paul was staring at his feet. Now and then he cast a quick glance at Costa. She wondered what he was thinking, wondered if he were recalling the dreadful night of the accident. And Nichos wasn't there as he usually was, always by his father's side. Perhaps he would not come to help out in the museum for a time; perhaps his mother wanted him close to her in the little house where there had once been two children.

Costa asked Paul and Lily if they would be happy to see their own country again. Paul only nodded, his eyes cast down.

He had turned away from his family to be with Jack. He had forsaken her. She didn't think she was angry about that anymore. She was puzzled by it. In a way, it interested her. It made her wonder if anyone would ever take up her whole attention the way Jack had Paul's.

In front of Paul, Jack had ignored her existence. But she and Jack had been alone together. That was her secret. She hadn't told Paul or anyone else that it had been she who had found Jack on the islet in the middle of the night. He had talked to her then. He had even laughed. Once.

Mr. Hemmings no longer danced for the Greeks at

Giorgi's taverna or, as far as she knew, in any other place in Limena. Jack hadn't been around since the death of Christos. Paul didn't speak his name, nor did she. She was looking at him, vaguely aware of her father struggling to say something in Greek, Costa murmuring encouragement. Paul turned his head toward her as if aware of her scrutiny. She smiled. She hadn't meant to; the smile had come to her lips without thought.

She kept looking at him when he'd turned away to stare at a far corner of the agora. He had smiled back at her, but his forehead had furrowed. He must be thinking all the time about everything that had happened here on Thasos. She believed he would think about her too, just as she thought about him. In some way, they would always hold each other in some corner of their minds.

"Lily, I hope you will come back to us here," Costa said to her.

She shook his small, hard hand, which touched the museum antiquities with reverence, which had clasped the shoulders of his boys with such gentleness.

A word came to her that she had used before only at the sight of a very small baby or a young animal. Sweet. Costa was full of sweetness. He smiled down at her. The burden of her feeling for him was so heavy at that moment, she was relieved when they left him to go on to the waterfront. There they found a young fisherman who would be able to help them with their luggage. She mused about Costa all the way home, past the police station and the House of the Turk, past the shrine of Dionysus, a crumbling ruin in the brilliant sunlight.

⌐⌐⌐⌐ The Coreys were standing on the wharf. Odysseus had helped Mr. Corey load their suitcases and books onto the deck of the *Maria*.

Lily was astonished at the number of people who had come to see them off. Even some of the store owners, usually busy at their counters at that early hour, were standing on the quay along with Efthymios-Onassis and Mr. Xenophon, Giorgi, Dimitrious, Stella, and Mr. and Mrs. Kalligas. At the outskirts of the group stood the handsome policeman in his beautifully pressed uniform, wearing his sunglasses. Mrs. Kalligas draped some crocheted doilies over Mrs. Corey's hands, and she put them into her Greek wool bag. Then, hurrying past her, Mr. Panakos came directly to Lily and told her to hold out her hand. When she did, he placed on her palm the tiny alabaster goat.

"Oh!" she exclaimed with delight. Mr. Panakos grinned. He didn't need a translation.

"You looked for so many months at him," he said, "that you must take him home with you." He stared at the goat, and for a second Lily thought she detected a faint regret on his face. Then he shrugged. "Good journey," he said, and walked rapidly across the quay to his shop.

Lily and Paul stood on the forward deck. She had been hugged flat, she felt. She looked up at the mountain that rose toward Panagia, at the house where they had lived, nearly hidden by trees except for its tiled roof, at the theater, and beyond it, the crest where the acropolis stood.

"I am glad we're going home," she said to Paul. "Are you?"

"Yes," he replied.

If she lived a lifetime on Thasos, she wondered if she would have been able to know it all—the mountains, the villages, Theologos, Kastro, Prinos, the ports they had not visited: Limenaria and Stavros and Skala Potamia. There were trees she did not know the names of, and flowers and birds. There were ghostly places where the ancients had left their cities and their temples, still buried, but which would be gradually brought into the light of day by the archaeologists.

"Will you miss it?" she asked.

Paul didn't answer. She turned to him and saw he was staring fixedly at something. She looked in the same direction. On the car ferry pier, a few hundred yards away, stood Mr. Hemmings, his hand resting on the handgrip of his motorcycle, two small suitcases by his side. Behind him stood Jack. No one had come to see them off. They looked solitary, hardly even together. Perhaps a fly lighted on his ear; something made Jack turn his head slightly. She saw his face as he recognized Paul. He didn't smile. He was as unmoving as a statue. Yet some emotion so troubled his face, he looked as if he were about to shout or cry. Abruptly, he turned his back.

She felt a rush of anger. Paul had shut her out for so long! Now Jack had done it to him. Good! She turned to her brother, meaning to say something—to tell him what an awful person he had chosen to be his friend. He was still staring at Jack Hemmings. His mouth was tightly closed. On his cheek there trembled a large tear. It caught the light as it hung there; it seemed to hold the colors of the clothes worn by the people waving to them on the wharf, the bright storefronts, the flowers in their pots and boxes; and in that second before it slid down his cheek and disappeared, she glimpsed, too, a world of feeling and of loss.

"Paul," she said softly, "let's go in now and get seats by the window."

He snuffled and swallowed loudly.

"All right," he said. "That's a good idea, Lily."

Yearling Books presents:
NEWBERY MEDAL-WINNING NOVELS

Great Books You'll Really Love

☐ 0-440-41794-5	DEAR MR. HENSHAW	Beverly Cleary	$3.99/$4.99
☐ 0-440-43180-8	FROM THE MIXED UP FILES OF MRS. BASIL E. FRANKWEILER	E. L. Konigsburg	$3.99/$4.99
☐ 0-440-44250-8	JOHNNY TREMAIN	Esther Forbes	$3.99/$4.99
☐ 0-440-43988-4	ISLAND OF THE BLUE DOLPHINS	Scott O'Dell	$3.99/$4.99
☐ 0-440-40327-8	NUMBER THE STARS	Lois Lowry	$3.99/$4.99
☐ 0-440-40865-2	MISSING MAY	Cynthia Rylant	$3.99/$4.99
☐ 0-440-40752-4	SHILOH	Phyllis Reynolds Naylor	$3.99/$4.99
☐ 0-440-40402-1	THE SLAVE DANCER	Paula Fox	$3.99/$4.99
☐ 0-440-49596-2	THE WITCH OF BLACKBIRD POND	Elizabeth George Speare	$3.99/$4.99
☐ 0-440-49805-8	A WRINKLE IN TIME	Madeleine L'Engle	$3.99/$4.99 U.S./Can.

Bantam Doubleday Dell
Books for Young Readers

Bantam Doubleday Dell Books for Young Readers
2451 South Wolf Road
Des Plaines, IL 60018

Please send the items I have checked above. I am enclosing $_____ (please add $2.50 to cover postage and handling). Send check or money order, no cash or C.O.D.s please.

Mr./Ms.
_____
Name

_____
Address

_____
City   State   Zip

BFYR 14 11/93

Please allow four to six weeks for delivery.
Prices and availability subject to change without notice.